Under the Bedclothes

Bump in the Night

In the Under the Bedclothes series:

The Screaming Field *Wendy Eyton*
Tales Told After Lights Out *Pat Thomson*

In the Nightmares series

Horrorscopes *Nicholas Adams*
IOU *Nicholas Adams*
Class Trip *Bebe Faas Rice*
Nightmare Inn *T. S. Rue*
Deadly Stranger *M. C. Sumner*
The Teacher *Joseph Locke*

STORIES UNDER THE BEDCLOTHES

BUMP IN THE NIGHT

Mary Hoffman

Illustrations by
George Buchanan

Lions

An Imprint of HarperCollins *Publishers*

First published in Great Britain in Lions 1993
3 5 7 9 8 6 4

Lions is an imprint of HarperCollins Children's Books,
a division of HarperCollins Publishers Ltd,
77–85 Fulham Palace Road,
Hammersmith, London W6 8JB

ISBN 0 00 674737-X

Printed and bound in Great Britain by
HarperCollins Manufacturing, Glasgow

CONTENTS

For the Coleridge "Class of 93"–
a good vintage – particularly Jessica,
Joanna, Stephron and Jack.

A Perfect Place

If we'd stayed on the motorway everything would have been different. But, as Dad said, who wants to spend a bank holiday on the motorway? Lots of people, going by the line of cars headed out of London that warm May Monday. We were supposed to be driving into Kent for a picnic in the "Garden of England" and there we were, stuck in a metal box on wheels on a road like any other you've ever seen. Not even the garden path of England. So we turned off the M2 and promptly got lost.

It wasn't Mum's fault, in spite of what Dad says. She's a very good navigator and gives clear directions, not like our grandma who says things like, "you turn left where that pub used to be that was burned down in the war". No, Mum was reading the map all right as we moved from A roads to B roads and then country lanes with passing places. But you know how it is with road atlases. Unless you've got a proper Ordnance Survey map, which we didn't have, once you get into the little villages, the roads don't seem to do what the nice clear orange lines on the map tell you they do.

"Look, there's a signpost," said Clare, my sister. "It says Little Huffington straight ahead, Wrotham and Morple to the left and Winningham to the right."

Mum consulted her map. "Well, Winningham's the only one I've got marked, so let's go there."

"It's not as if we wanted to go anywhere in particular," I said, which I wished later I hadn't. "Anywhere will do, if we're just looking for somewhere pretty to have a picnic."

Our quests for the perfect picnic place are famous. We all want the same thing – a smooth stretch of grass without stones, nettles or cowpats, preferably beside a tinkling stream or river, with no other people around. Usually we end up eating in the back of the car in a lay-by and then, as we drive sadly home, we see the perfect picnic place half a mile away, looking like something on one of Granny's jigsaw puzzles.

Today was different, though. We had all the car windows down because of the heat, and the air smelt sweet with hawthorn from the hedges. The little road to Winningham suddenly ran out of tarmac and we were jolting over dirt-track, full of potholes and pebbles.

"Oh, my poor suspension," groaned Dad, and then we heard an awful grinding noise and the car stopped.

There is nothing worse than grown-ups arguing over whose fault something is, so I'll spare you the description of what followed. Anyway, we all got out of the car and decided to walk to the nearest village to see if we could phone for help. No one wanted to stay behind in the car in the heat. We left the picnic in the boot, which was our first mistake – or our second, if you count leaving the motorway in the first place.

It was quite a pleasant walk. Round about here you could see what people meant by the "Garden of England". There were hedges on both sides of the lane, but they were mainly hawthorn, as I said, and full of creamy white flowers with a heavenly smell. Through the gaps in the hedges you could see fields and meadows covered with wild flowers. The air was full of the sounds of birds singing and the buzzing of bees, and we saw millions of butterflies.

"It's not so bad." said Mum. "You know, I think it looks very promising along here for our picnic."

"Huh!" said Dad, still trying to be cross about the car, but you could see he was softening.

Suddenly the hedges gave way and we were at the top of a little hill. At the bottom of it nestled a village – it was the kind of village that can only be described as "nestling". I think we all gasped. It was full of thatched cottages, most of them whitewashed with black wooden beams on the outside and a tiny grey church with a square tower. Most of the houses and the church were set round a triangular green which sparkled like an emerald from the top of the hill. Along one side of the triangle ran a clear fast-flowing river, and the road from the church to an inn on the other side of the green crossed it by a little wooden bridge.

As we stood, spellbound, we saw people coming out of the inn in fancy dress.

"Morris dancers," cried Dad. "Now if that doesn't make a perfect English village scene, I don't know what does! Let's go back and get the picnic basket. We'll never find a better spot than this!"

A Perfect Place

If only we'd agreed! But Clare and I thought we'd miss the dancers if we went back and Mum persuaded him to stick to the original plan. They could go back for the basket when we'd used the phone. But as we walked down into the village, we could see no phonebox. There was no shop either and not a car or garage in sight.

"I'll have to go into the pub," said Dad, happily.

Mum snorted. "Well, bring us all something to drink out here and we'll watch the Morris dancers. I'm parched after that walk."

We sat on a little stone wall at the edge of the green while Dad went into the inn. It was very old-fashioned looking, with thick greenish glass in the windows. The sign outside said "The Kinges Armes", but though it had oldy-worldy spelling it looked quite new, as if the pub might have been called something else before.

The Morris dancing was terrific. It wasn't just men with sticks and hankerchiefs and bells round their knees, though I like that kind too. It was more like a play really. There was Robin Hood and Maid Marian – you could recognize them easily enough, though Maid Marian was obviously a young man dressed up. There was a dragon and a hobby-horse and a fool who went round with a large soup-ladle asking for money. We were so absorbed in the story that we hadn't noticed Dad coming out with the drinks. He was holding four tankards made of grey metal and he looked a bit worried.

"What's the matter, love? Didn't you get through?" asked Mum.

"No. They said they didn't have a phone. At least I think that's what they said. The local accent's very strong round here. I could hardly make them out."

"Well, never mind. Sit and have your drink till the dance is over. Then we can try somewhere else."

"They gave me the drinks on the house," said Dad, passing out the tankards. "I hope it's all right for the girls. They didn't have any Coke or lemonade – they're all drinking this stuff. I think it's mead."

"Must be some sort of local festival," said Mum, sipping her drink.

I tasted mine. It was very strong, sort of bitter and sweet at the same time, with a lovely smell of honey. It wasn't as good as an ice-cold can of something soft, but I got to like it after the first few sips. I was watching the dancers. There was one in particular who caught my eye. He was dressed all in red and yellow, a bit like the Pied Piper and he was as lithe and graceful as a ballet dancer. He had long brown curls with flowers twined in them and he carried several brightly-coloured scarves which he wove into wild patterns around him as he danced. He seemed to be the leader because, after a while, he danced off the green and over the wooden bridge and all the others followed him. He danced through the lych gate of the church and in and out of the grave-stones, all the others following him, banging drums and blowing pipes. I was afraid the vicar would come out and shout at them, but everyone seemed to take it for granted.

When the dance was over, the dancers all came and got drinks of mead from the pub and sat round the edge of the green while other entertain-ers came out. Only the hobby horse couldn't sit down because of his costume sticking out in front and behind, so he had to stay standing up. We had completely forgotten about the car and the AA. This was the best bit of country life we had ever found on our day trips out. There were jugglers and tumblers and fire-eaters and we sat with the sun burning on our backs and the mead slipping pleasantly down our throats.

Presently I noticed the young handsome dancer sitting practically at my feet. He looked up and smiled. "Good morrow, mistress," he said, pluck-ing a flower out of his hair and offering it to me.

11

"Good morrow," I said back, feeling an awful nerd, because there I was in my jeans and T-shirt, with my hair all messy, and there was this drop-dead gorgeous bloke of at least seventeen giving me a flower.

"Are you enjoying the entertainment?" he said. "It is a merry Maying, is it not?"

I thought he was taking the Mickey but I was determined to play it cool. "Watch this one," he said and I saw a fire-eater put a hot coal in his mouth. Then two other men came with bellows and blew on it till it was red hot. I felt myself sweating. Then someone put some sort of shell on top of the coal and it bubbled and split open.

"Oh, what is it?" I asked the dancer.

"He broileth an oyster in his mouth," he laughed.

"But that's impossible," I protested.

I was beginning to feel that everything was unreal. At first I thought it came from drinking strong mead on a warm day, but then I started noticing things that were strange about the village. There were no television aerials and no telegraph wires, no streetlamps and no traffic lights. Strangest of all, everyone was in fancy dress, not just the Morris dancers. And somehow, it didn't look like fancy dress on them. The clothes weren't new; they looked as if they wore them all the time. All the men had long hair too, though some of them did look as if they were wearing curly wigs. The children all wore long dresses – even the little boys looked as if they were wearing skirts under their long coats. I suddenly thought it was a very hot day for a village to choose to do dressing-up.

I jumped down off the wall and went over to Dad, who was mesmerised, watching something like a Punch and Judy show.

"Dad!" I said, tugging at his shirtsleeve. "There's something fishy about this village. There's nothing modern here."

He stared like a sleepwalker. "What, love? Oh, yes, you mean all the costumes. I think they must be having a festival, or maybe this is one of those places where people come to act out battles of Roundheads and Cavaliers."

That was what it reminded me of!

"Then this lot are Cavaliers," I said. We'd done them for a project at school and I remembered the plumed hats and lace collars and cuffs.

"It's not just the clothes, Dad. Remember they said they didn't have a phone? That's a bit unlikely for a pub, isn't it?"

Then I noticed the innkeeper. He had come out of The Kinges Armes and was standing with his arms crossed, just looking at our family.

Suddenly, I knew that we had to get out of that village or we would be in some sort of terrible danger. I don't know what made me feel like this – perhaps it was the effects of the mead – but I had a dreadful premonition of something awful about to happen. Goodness knows how I managed to convince the others that it was time to go (my memories of this are a bit muzzy), but perhaps they all felt something was amiss too, because before long (we'd all finished our drinks anyway) we were all getting on our feet and thinking about the best way to go to find the nearest phone.

Then the innkeeper stepped forward. He was an odd-looking man, and I felt uneasy just looking at him. He said something like, "You must stay for the banquet."

Mum thanked him. "You're very kind," she said, "but we've got a picnic lunch back in the car."

The innkeeper looked at her as if she were a Martian.

"Tuna fish sandwiches," said Clare, helpfully, but he still looked blank.

"I insist," he said, sort of showing us through the pub to a garden at the back. I suppose Clare and I are so used to gardens at the back of pubs that we didn't think it seemed strange or spooky. Only this one didn't have colourful umbrellas and a climbing frame for littlies. It was full of long wooden tables and benches. There were lots of dishes laid out and more jugs of mead. All the villagers and Morris dancers crowded in behind us. Dad's eyes lit up when he saw all the food. His tummy is his weakness, Mum says.

"Well, this is right smashing. It'd be a shame not to join in, wouldn't it, love?"

"It would a shame to waste that picnic I got up early to make," said Mum, but she could see she wasn't going to get Dad to eat tuna fish sandwiches when there were these groaning boards on offer.

"Don't fuss, pet," he said. "We can have the picnic for our tea. You couldn't find a more perfect place for lunch than this."

It was a good lunch too, though I couldn't recognize all the dishes. There were a lot of pies and pasties and I wasn't sure what kind of meat they had in them but they tasted OK. Conversation was uphill work till my red and yellow dancer turned up and slid in beside me at the bench.

"Aha!" said the innkeeper. "You are honoured, mistress, to be the choice of the Lord."

I looked at the young dancer. All that and a Lord too? I suppose someone must have given me more mead to drink, because I felt very peculiar.

Yet at the back of my mind a little voice kept on asking what this wonderful man was doing paying attention to a scruffy kid like me. He gave me a beautiful smile and I saw that one of his front teeth was chipped. "I am the Lord of Misrule, lady," he said. "King for a day of our May ceremonies."

"Aye," said the innkeeper, bustling about with trays and dishes, "and highly honoured we are, to have his young Lordship all the way from Winningham."

"I thought this was Winningham," said Mum.

All the people at our table laughed merrily.

"Oh no, mistress," said the innkeeper. "We are nowhere so big and fine as that. This is Little Cossington."

Mum frowned, and I could see she was thinking that wasn't on her map either; of course it was a very *small* village.

"Try some of this, mistress," said the Lord of Misrule, handing me a dish that looked like a mound of gooseberries. He dug a long-handled spoon into the middle of it and I could see it was full of rich, sweet-smelling cream. It was delicious. It was such a hot afternoon and I had drunk so much mead that I felt as if I was dreaming. So when the young Lord leant over and brought his face close to mine and I knew he was going to kiss me, I just sat there thinking, "This can't be real". I closed my eyes.

Then Clare shrieked, "Sally! Don't let him touch you!" and everything went strange. I must have passed out. When I came round I was lying on the ground and there was no one there but my family. Not just no people, but no tables and benches either, just a field or something.

"Where am I?" I asked, in the time-honoured fashion. "What happened?"

"I don't know," said Dad. "One minute we were all eating and drinking in the pub garden and the next Clare screamed and now we're all alone in the middle of a field."

"Why did you yell like that, Clare?" asked Mum.

"That dancer, the one who looked like the Pied Piper," said Clare, who was deathly white under her freckles, "he was going to kiss Sally. And she was going to let him."

"Well," said Dad. "You're quite right that she's too young for that sort of thing, but . . . ."

"You don't understand!" interrupted Clare. "As he came closer to her I could see that he didn't have a proper face at all. It was a skull!"

There was silence for a minute, then Mum

said, in classic understatement, "There was something I didn't like about that village from the word go!"

"Let's find the car," said Dad and we all set out in what we thought was the direction of the village green. Within a few yards we were out of the field and staring silently at the triangular patch of grass. At each of its three corners there was a huge mature horse-chestnut tree, laden with either pink or white candles. There was no sign of a river and there was not a house or any other building in sight. The green was being used as a roundabout and there were road markings and a signpost for Winningham. As we stood at the edge of the field a car honked a warning to us as it sped past. I expect we looked dozy enough to walk straight in front of it.

We crossed the roundabout and walked back up the lane to where we had left our car. It was all different now, no meadows and sweet-smelling hedges, no butterflies, no birdsong.

Across the countryside marched the huge pylons that we normally never noticed. Strangest of all, about three hundred yards before our car, when we could already see it in the distance; there was a garage set back from the road. We turned into it and Dad spoke to the mechanic, who went off with him.

Mum bought us some cold drinks from the shop. I had a terrible headache, so I went to the Ladies and splashed my face with cold water. When I got back, Mum was asking the woman in the shop if she knew a village in the neighbourhood called Little Cossington. There was an uncomfortable pause before the woman replied, "Why do you want to know?"

Imagine my surprise when Mum said, "My daughter here's been doing a project on the seventeenth century. She heard there was something special about a village somewhere near here."

The woman laughed. "Special? That's a way of putting it, I suppose. Still, the person you want to talk to about Little Cossington is the vicar of Winningham. He's written a book about it."

By the time we'd finished our drinks, Dad was back with the car in working order and we all felt better. Mum was determined to solve the mystery then and there, so we drove slowly past the deserted green of what was left of our perfect village and took the road to Winningham.

The vicarage was right next to the church in Winningham, which was certainly much bigger than Little Cossington. It had a shop too and a post office and a video hire shop, which made Mum wince. Winningham was definitely *not* the sort of place we usually considered for a picnic spot.

The vicar was at home. In fact, he was sitting reading a day-old Sunday paper in his front garden. He was not too pleased to be disturbed on his day off, but as soon as Mum mentioned Little Cossington, he changed completely and asked us all in. We went into his little study, crammed with books and papers, and he shifted a few so that we could find somewhere to sit. When we were all perched on some sort of surface, he pulled a pamphlet out of one of the bookcases and handed it solemnly to Mum. It was called *The Plague Villages of Kent* by the Reverend Arthur Boniface, Vicar of Winningham.

"You'll find what you are looking for on page fifteen," he said. "Perhaps you had better read it out loud." This is what Mum read:

"'One of the most tragic stories of the Great Plague in Kent is the case of Little Cossington. It was a small community, neighbouring my present parish of Winningham. The villagers' lives would have been the hard one of a small agricultural community. Their everyday routine of labour in the fields and with their livestock during all the daylight hours was relieved and enlivened only by their regular rural and religious festivals. The year in Little Cossington was punctuated not only by the high points of the church's year, such as Christmas, Easter and Whitsun, but also by traditional celebrations such as Harvest.

"'But by far the most important and looked forward to of all the village's fairs and festivals was their Mayday celebrations. We learn from contemporary accounts that the villagers of Little Cossington did not go in for a maypole, but devoted that day to feasting and to mumming, dancing, and other forms of entertainment. They always elected a Lord of Misrule, someone who was "King for a Day", a leader of the revels, who was licensed to do whatever he liked. Because Little Cossington was a small community and there were few people to take part in the revels on Mayday, many travellers journeyed to the village to take part in the entertainment or simply to watch it.

"'And this, sadly, proved the downfall of Little Cossington. In the spring of 1665, which was uncommonly warm, they had chosen as their Lord of Misrule a young man from the larger village of Winningham. It was supposed to be George Medway, a farmer's son, but on the day of the celebrations, Gervase of Ashenden, who was son to the local squire and landowner, persuaded him to let him take his place. A bag of money changed hands and Gervase, who was of much the same build as George, changed clothes, donned a mask and came to Little Cossington with Death as his attendant.

"'For young Gervase was just back from a trip to London and had caught the Plague, though he did not know it as yet. He danced the day away in feverish gaiety at Little Cossington and used his privilege as Lord of Misrule to flirt with all the village girls. Who knows how many conquests Gervase made as George? But he did not live to harvest the crop of hearts he set beating faster that last mad May day in the village.

"'Before he left, he kissed the innkeeper's daughter, a pretty little maid of not more than twelve years old – and that is how the plague came to Little Cossington.'"

There was a long silence in the stuffy little room, broken eventually by Clare.

"And was he sorry, the red and yellow one?"

The vicar looked at her shrewdly.

"The Lord of Misrule did indeed wear a red and yellow costume, though I did not mention it in my account. Yes, he realized what he had done, when he lay on his deathbed. The inn-keeper of the King's Arms came to see him, mad with grief over his little daughter and already infected with his own death, and cursed the young

Lord as he lay tossing with the fever."

"What did he say?" I asked, my mouth feeling dry.

"He said he would pray every remaining hour of his life and after death, if he was able, that Gervase of Ashenden would never know peace in the afterlife but would dance for all eternity before he would find another maid willing to abide his kiss. His very words, recorded by a predecessor of mine, the incumbent of Winningham over three hundred years ago."

"I don't think any of them found peace," said Dad quietly.

"The village green was dug into a great pit where the victims were all buried," said the Reverend Boniface, "and in later years horse-chestnut trees were planted round it, in accordance with the belief that they keep off pestilence. The children come from miles around to collect the conkers in the autumn."

"What about Gervase?" I asked. I couldn't bear to think of his crooked smile and how nearly he had kissed me.

"He requested that he be buried alongside the villagers whose life he had blighted," said the vicar, "and that no memorial should be raised to him. The Ashendens had no other heir and their line died out. However, George Medway's descendents lived and thrived and now live in the Manor House themselves. The current head of the family owns a large chain of supermarkets."

We went back to the car. We didn't stop as we passed the green at what had been Little Cossington. It was late in the afternoon and the horse chestnut trees cast long slanting shadows over the grass.

Rest in peace, Gervase, I thought. *Perhaps there will be a girl brave enough one day.*

"I don't think I'll ever want to go for another picnic," said Mum, "I don't want to find a perfect place ever again."

"Here," said Dad, "talking of picnics. Let's stop at the first lay-by we come to and get that hamper out. I don't feel as if I've had anything to eat all day!"

Bump in the Night

Ellie fumed all the way to Gloucestershire. Her anger was the only thing that kept her going through the long, cold railway journey. She munched sullenly on the sandwiches and cake her mother had given her, but it didn't make up for Mum not being there.

"How could she do this to me?" she thought for the hundredth time, glaring at the kindly middle-aged lady sitting opposite, who had promised Mum she would keep an eye on Ellie till the train got to Kemble. "It's not even as if he likes me. He only puts up with me because of Mum. Three days with Him! And at Christmas too!"

She had said all this often enough to Mum but

it had done no good. A crisis had come up at work and Mum couldn't get away till Christmas Eve. Ellie would just have to go down by train and stay with Donald and his son till Mum joined them. His son! A smaller version of Donald, she supposed gloomily, with glasses and a miniature tweed jacket. Why did they have to have Christmas with them anyway? They'd always been all right on their own before. Because she's going to marry him, a little voice at the back of her mind said, and Ellie looked so fierce that the lady opposite huddled into her winter coat and thought that the odd little girl looked as if she could take care of herself.

The journey passed in silence till they reached Kemble and the lady helped Ellie out with her suitcase. As she waved through the window, she noticed the fair-haired man in the tweed jacket meeting the child at the barrier and looked puzzled. The mother had been blond too.

"There you are! You must be frozen!" Donald was determined to to be as hearty and bearlike as necessary to to make up for Ellie's iciness. "Nick's stayed in the car out of the cold," he said, fussing round with her bag and his keys. Ellie looked round the station. There were no black or even brown faces on the platform. Perhaps there were none in the whole of Gloucestershire? She felt very out of place and homesick for London. And there was nothing for her to do except climb into the car behind Donald and Nick. She felt like Kay in the Snow Queen, with a sliver of cold hatred in her heart for the pair of them.

Nick said nothing but hello on the journey to the cottage. Donald rabbited on about how there'd be snow before Christmas and how they'd waited for Ellie before bringing in the tree. He drove erratically, turning his head round dangerously to talk to her.

It was already dark and they were soon far away from any streetlights and the comforting glow of lots of living-rooms. Ellie had never been so deep into the country before. It seemed to be nothing but winding lanes and dark menacing trees. The car headlights cut a yellow path through the countryside, making the car feel like a safe cocoon hurtling through the hostile unknown. Ellie thought miserably that no matter how much she disliked Donald and was prepared to dislike Nick, she would rather be inside the car with them than outside on her own.

"Here we are at last," said Donald cheerfully as they scrunched up a short drive outside a garage. The cottage was the middle one of three, set on a hillside in the middle of the woods – in the middle of nowhere. Ellie noticed the grey stones illuminated by an outside lantern, a wooden front door with an old-fashioned latch. And then they stepped inside a Christmas card. She couldn't help herself; she gasped.

"It's lovely," she said stiffly, looking at the log fire, the rocking chair, the rag-rug and the comfortable grey tabby on it. Donald had knocked the downstairs rooms of his cottage into one so that it was very big, but it was still cosy. There was a large sofa opposite the fire, which divided the room back into two again, and at the far end was a grandfather clock, a bureau and a dining table and chairs.

"Put some logs on the fire, Nick," said Donald briskly. "I want to show Ellie her room." He opened a cupboard door at the side of the fireplace and Ellie thought, you must be joking! But it revealed a tiny staircase. Donald had to bend almost double to carry her case up it.

"I hope you'll like this little cubbyhole," he said and Ellie thought he looked anxious to please, like a big dog who knows you prefer cats.

She loved it and her face softened. It was a very small room, just big enough to hold a single bed and a white chest-of-drawers. There were some hooks on the back of the door and a tiny window with a broad wooden sill on the inside. It looked over the front garden, now black outside the window, with just a glow from the outside light.

Ellie swallowed. "Thank you, Donald," she said. "I like it very much."

"Good, good" he beamed. "Now, you make yourself at home and I'll go and get supper out of the Aga." He half fell down the little stairs and Ellie pulled off her coat and hung it on one of the hooks. She tugged her woolly hat off her mass of black curls and sighed. The room was warm from the fire below; its chimney took up the whole of one wall.

Then she heard Nicholas's voice, sounding as if it were right in her ear.

"Right little barrel of fun, isn't she?"

"Give her a chance, Nick – she doesn't know us. And she's missing her mother," came Donald's voice, lower but equally distinct.

Ellie realized that the voices were floating up the chimney. She hunched her shoulders and frowned. She'd show them.

The dinner table was laid for three. There was a steaming savoury casserole and baked potatoes with lots of butter and pepper. Ellie sat with her back to the fire, feeling the heat while the front of her was hit by the coldness at that end of the room. Nick ate silently, wolfing down huge amounts. Ellie had to smile at her image of him as a small Donald. Although only thirteen, he was as tall as his father, though not as broad. His tousled mousey hair and thin hawklike face made him look quite unlike Donald, who was all thickness and solidity – hair a blond-grey thatch, features strong and vivid.

"I am quite out of place here," thought Ellie. "These people belong here. I just look like a bandit they've brought in for questioning."

In fact, she looked more like a pirate, with her dark skin, black hair and gold earrings. She took after her father, which was her bad luck, because he had disappeared before she was born and she grew up with her fair, blonde mum, who was always being asked whose baby she was looking after.

Donald was thinking, "What a beautiful child she is! Sitting at my table like a wild bird, not trusting me, but needing me whether she likes it or not."

Nick thought. "She hates us both. Dad's kidding himself if he thinks she'll accept him marrying Kathy."

Ellie could hardly keep her eyes open after supper. Donald draw the sofa up closer to the fire and installed her there with a cup of frothy cocoa.

"You can help with the dishes from tomorrow," he said, "but be a guest tonight."

The grey cat jumped on to her lap and started
to knead Ellie's jeans. Ellie hardly had the energy
to stumble up the stairs to the bathroom before
coming back through to the living-room and up
to her own little eyrie. But she was awake enough
to notice Nick disappearing into another little
cupboard by the fireplace. His stairs must have
gone higher then hers, though, because she soon
heard him thumping about overhead. He must
have the whole attic for himself. She was too tired
to think about it any more. She snuggled under
the duvet and fell asleep straight away.

And woke – to the pitch blackness and the
creak of the stairs outside her door. Ellie suddenly
knew what it meant when people said their hearts
were in their mouths. She clapped a hand over
her lips to keep it in.

But nothing happened. No one lifted the latch
and crept stealthily in. Gradually Ellie relaxed.
She could hear the faint distant sound of Nick's
breathing, and her heart climbed back down to
where it belonged. The creaks went on, together
with a whole orchestra of different sounding
creaks and cracks from down in the living room.
It was just the sound of wood growing cold and
shrinking as the heat from the dead fire left the
room. Whoever said the country was quiet?
thought Ellie, as she lay back in her bed. An owl

shrieked, a vixen barked and then the outlines of the room appeared in the greyness and a choir of unreasonably pleased birds started to sing carols.

It seemed only minutes later that Donald called up that breakfast was ready. Indeed it wasn't really very long, because this was the shortest day of the year and the dawn came very late.

"It'll be dark by half past three," said Donald. "We'll get the tree in this morning and you two can decorate it this evening. I'll have to do some shopping this afternoon."

Ellie eyed Nick warily. Donald had made a big pot of porridge and left it overnight in the cool oven of the Aga. It had turned brown on the top, but the inside was a wonderful thick, creamy mixture. Ellie had thought it looked horrible but had to admit it tasted lovely, particularly with lots of dark brown sugar, and cream. Donald had his good points, she was beginning to realize. He could cook, he knew how to make a house homely and he was very kind. "Make someone a wonderful wife," she thought grimly, eating her third helping of porridge.

But Nick was a different matter, silent, as suspicious of her as she was of him and, if not hostile, not friendly either. She was so glad she hadn't made a fool of herself by screaming out in the night. She didn't fancy playing brothers and sisters with him, putting tinsel on a Christmas tree. As if they could ever look like brother and sister. As if Donald could ever look like her father, come to that.

Her heart ached for her real father, whom she had never seen. He had gone back to St Lucia, her mum had said, and all she knew about him was that he was tall and handsome and her mother had fallen head over heels in love with him at first sight.

Ellie washed up in the old-fashioned kitchen, while Nick and Donald went to get jackets and wellingtons.

"Want to come?" asked Nick, who was carrying an axe.

"Where are you going?" said Ellie.

"To cut the tree, of course," said Nick sharply. "Dad told you."

"But can you just do that? Won't you get in trouble?"

"Not in our own woods," grinned Nick.

Ellie didn't want to go. She would feel even more out of place now she knew that Donald owned the woodland behind the cottage. She would stay safe and warm indoors with the Aga and the cat. She watched the two of them from the kitchen window, climbing the almost vertical slope outside the back door until they disappeared among the trees, laughing, their breath coming out in puffs of steam.

They were back before long, stamping earth off their boots and chopping little branches off the bottom of the tree in the back yard. Donald brought in a bucket of earth weighted with stones and put it on newspaper at the end of the living-room away from the fire. Then the two of them carried in the fir tree. It must have looked a small one out in the woods, but inside the house it was huge, as tall as the clock. It brought with it a sharp, resiny smell that made Ellie want to cry.

The room was still full of it when they all got back from shopping in Cirencester. Ellie had received some curious looks in the shops. That's how it would always be if Mum married Donald and they came to live here. Everyone would think she was adopted.

"It'll snow before bedtime," said Donald, stoking up the log fire. "Let's unpack the shopping and rustle up a quick supper. Then you two can get going with the tree."

Nick pulled the curtains. It was already quite dark outside. The shortest day – you didn't really notice that sort of thing in the city. There were always plenty of lights in the streets and the shops. Ellie put on another jumper and helped Donald put away the shopping. He made huge

Spanish omelettes with onions and potatoes and all sorts of odds and ends, and they had great chunks of French bread with them. Ellie had never eaten so much in her life as she was doing here. She'd have to watch it or she'd need new clothes. Donald cleared the table and Nick brought down some boxes from the attic.

Ellie thought of the Christmas tree things at home, which wouldn't be used this year. "It'd be a waste, having a tree when we're not going to be here," her mum had said. Ellie remembered the golden bird with the red glass eyes and thought of it lying in its tissue paper, along with the little wooden rocking-horse and the glittering butterflies. None of them would have Christmas this year. She blinked back a tear. Nick was looking at her, almost sympathetically.

"You choose the things," he said. "I'll put up the high ones you can't reach."

Donald and Nick's decorations were lots of coloured tinsel and balls and some unusual things too, like a set of Chinese lanterns with red tassels dangling underneath them and a whole flight of fragile paper birds that opened out and clipped back on themselves.

"Those were Mum's idea," said Nick, gently unfolding a pink bird with a turquoise body.

Ellie looked up in surprise. She had never once

35

thought about Nick's mother. For a moment, she thought that he might feel about Donald and her mum the same way she did. They exchanged tentative smiles.

"They're lovely," said Ellie, stroking a bird with a long green tail, "really pretty."

Donald topped the tree off with a shiny gold star. "It really makes this end of the room come alive, doesn't it?" he said with satisfaction, looking at the noble tree sparkling and glittering like a Queen without a court.

Mum phoned later that evening and Ellie spoke to her. "How are you getting on, darling?" her voice crackled down the line.

"Fine," said Ellie. "We've decorated the tree."

"Good. You're making yourself at home, then?"

"Donald's doing that."

"Only two more days, darling, then I'll be with you."

"I miss you, Mum."

"Me too. Be good."

Ellie didn't think any creaks would wake her tonight. But no one could have slept through the crash from downstairs. Nick came down his cupboard-staircase as fast as Ellie did down hers. The living room felt strange, tingling as if something very exciting had just happened. One of the dining-chairs was on its side. The grey cat was hiding under the table.

"Must have been Figaro," said Nick, righting the chair.

Ellie sank on to the sofa. The room still tingled. She could feel there was more to it than a cat. The tree stood at the far end, bedecked and beautiful, surrounded by the cottage's solid old furniture, yet Ellie had the strangest feeling that everything in the room was holding its breath, like children playing "statues" at a party.

Nick kicked the logs back into life and sat down next to her. "My mum always used to say that when she was a little girl, she never believed a room stood still when she went out of it. She was always trying to rush back in and surprise it – catch everything moving around."

"I know what she meant," said Ellie. Then, "Nick, what happened to your mum?"

"She went away," said Nick. "Ran off with someone else – I haven't seen her since I was six."

"My dad ran away, too," said Ellie. "Not with anyone else, but a long way away. He didn't want a baby, my mum says."

"I don't think my mum did either," said Nick. He turned to Ellie in the firelight. "We're a right pair, aren't we?"

"But Mum wanted me," protested Ellie.

"And Dad wanted me," said Nick. "I think he wants you too."

Ellie tried to digest this.

"He always wanted a daughter," said Nick. "And he really likes your mum, you know."

"Yes, I know," sighed Ellie. "She really likes him too. They even look a bit alike. You could be their son. It's only me that'd be the odd one out."

"You really believe that, don't you?" said Nick. "Well, I think you'd better go and sleep on it. But ask yourself who *feels* more like a dad to you, my dad, or some guy who ran away when he knew you were coming?"

Before she got back into bed, Ellie looked out of the window. The world had an unearthly light to it. She opened the latch and leant out, catching an unmistakable almost metallic taste on the night air. The snow had come.

In the morning the living room looked ordinary again, but Ellie went and looked closely at all the furniture. She asked Donald about it. The bureau was made of walnut, the chair and tables of oak and the grandfather clock was rosewood. That set her thinking – furniture made out of roses? It was amazing how you could forget that wood had once been trees. Every bit of furniture had once been growing in a wood or forest.

That day they all went for a long walk in the snow. Nick lent her an old pair of his boots, but she still had to wear three pairs of socks to fit them on. It was bitterly cold and they met no one else.

"We could be a dad out with his son and daughter," thought Ellie, "as long as no one else was looking."

She was sleepier than ever that evening. Country air, huge meals and interrupted nights combined to send her early to bed. She feel asleep to the sounds of Donald and Nick's voices rumbling up the chimney.

". . . accepting us now . . ."

". . . can't be easy . . ."

". . . mustn't cling on to the past . . ."

"Cling on to the past", said a voice in her dreams. It was the tree, but it looked like a tall women in a dark green dress, fantastically draped with necklaces, bracelets and rings. She stood amid a circle of other trees. Ellie knew they were a walnut, some rose trees and an oak but she had never seen a walnut tree before. They were all out in the snowy woods, dancing and singing, free and happy.

Through the woods came a tall dark man. Ellie wasn't afraid of him; she had dreamt about him often. He lifted her up on his shoulders so she could see the gold star that the tree-woman was wearing in her hair. It turned into a red and gold bird and flew away. Ellie struggled to get down; she must follow it. The man lowered her to the ground and she saw that his face had changed and it was Donald looking at her, and she was crying.

Ellie woke feeling cold. Her duvet had fallen off. Her watch said 6.15. She crept downstairs and lifted the latch. The room was tingling again. And the grandfather clock was six inches closer to the bureau than it had been yesterday! The tree ornaments jingled and tinkled, though there was no breeze in the room.

"Do you believe in ghosts?" she asked Nick when they had collected kindling from the woods. It was all damp and they had to brush it clear of snow and stack it in the outhouse next to the logs. Donald was busy sawing up a fallen tree.

"I don't *not* believe in them," he replied. "I just haven't seen one."

"But they wouldn't have to be people, would they?" said Ellie, "I mean, look at all this wood. It's sort of the ghost of trees, isn't it? And furniture too."

"Well, the bodies of trees," said Nick, "corpses of copses. You couldn't say it was ghosts unless it was more sort of . . . alive."

"Maybe that's what your mum meant about

rooms changing around when you go out of them? Furniture coming alive."

They went in for lunch, their fingers and toes tingling painfully in the warm kitchen.

"Well, Kathy will be here tomorrow," said Donald, heating up homemade soup on the Aga. "You'll be glad to see her, won't you, Ellie?"

Ellie didn't answer straightaway. Of course she wanted her mother here; wasn't that what she'd been so angry about for so long? Now, all of a sudden, she felt that she and Donald and Nick were an inner circle and Mum would be an outsider. It felt very strange.

That night the dream came back, but it was different. Ellie danced madly with the trees until the tall man came and lifted her up. When the bird flew away, Ellie let it go. The man who set her down on the snow was still Donald but he was smiling. The trees around the the bedizened fir stopped dancing and took root. Slowly they changed into pieces of furniture. She woke to find herself on the living-room floor without knowing how she got there. She had the strangest sensation for a minutes that the clock was bending over her with its big round face, then it blurred into Donald.

"I heard a crash," he said. "What are you doing down here, Ellie?"

"I must have sleepwalked," she said.

He picked her up in his arms and tried to carry her to her room but stopped, laughing, as he bumped his head on the cupboard-stairs.

"You'll have to manage on your own," he said, rubbing his head. He looked so comical, standing there in his pyjamas, without his glasses, his hair all standing on end. Ellie looked at her watch; it was already seven o'clock.

"It's Christmas Eve," she said. "Mum's coming today."

"I know," said Donald. "Happy Christmas Eve."

"The name's Ellie," said Ellie, disappearing up the stairs.

She heard Nick come rushing into the living room.

"What's all the racket, Dad?"

"I don't believe it," said Donald's voice up the chimney. "She just made a joke. I think it's going to be all right."

Ellie smiled to herself. She could hear the grandfather clock ticking away and she wondered if it was thinking of the days when it was a whole rose garden. Everything was more than it seemed from the outside.

Foxy Lady

"There is nothing to beat an English hunt in full cry when it comes to colour and spectacle . . ."

Haydn pressed the mute button on the remote control and cut off the reporter's toadying voice. The TV picture cut from galloping horses and running hounds to the reporter himself, his breath steaming on the cold morning air. He looked serious and Haydn knew he had got to the "But some people think it is a barbaric activity . . ." part of his story. Haydn had seen it all before. He only took the mute off when the camera turned to the saboteurs. Outfox was the local group of animal activists dedicated to stopping the Todwood Hunt. Every time it set out from outside the Fox & Hounds, Outfox was there.

The reporter was thrusting his microphone into the face of Olivia Hamilton, one of the most active saboteurs. Haydn sat up. He really admired Olivia, who came from a local county family just as aristocratic as Lord and Lady Todwood's. She was also very beautiful, even in a padded anorak on a cold winter's morning. Her red hair tumbled to her shoulders and her vivid face lit up the TV screen as she gave her reasons for opposing the hunt. "Well, thank you, Ms Hamilton," said the slimy reporter, "Or actually, shouldn't it be the *Honourable* Ms Hamilton?" He made it sound like an insult and Olivia made an impatient gesture to show how unimportant that was. "So there we have it," the reporter said, turning to the camera. "The saboteurs are led by a renegade from the hunting classes themselves and, if I may say so, one extremely foxy lady."

Haydn wondered if the reporter would have such a self-satisfied grin if he knew the rude sign Olivia was making behind his back. The camera drew back and panned over the Fox & Hounds stableyard. Haydn could just spot himself handing out leaflets. He sighed and pressed the off button. He looked such a little kid among those tall horses and the other Outfox members. His parents only let him go to the meet if he promised to do nothing except hand out protest leaflets. He wasn't supposed even to get into arguments. He couldn't wait to be grown up and be interviewed on TV – he wouldn't let them patronise *him*. Still, he reckoned it was Olivia who had made the reporter look silly, not the other way round.

He glanced at the clock – 6.10. He'd better put the kettle on. Mum would soon be back from her job at Todwood Hall. He was dreading the day when Lady Todwood found out he was with Outfox. What would he do if Mum said she'd lose her job if he carried on supporting the saboteurs? Haydn hated her working up at the Hall, cleaning and shopping for the likes of Lord and Lady Todwood, but his dad had been out of work for two years, ever since the electronics factory closed, and Haydn was too young even to get a Saturday job. He didn't mind having Dad around the house most of the time. It was specially good in the holidays and at weekends when they could go bird-spotting or badger-watching. It was because Dad was as keen on animals as Haydn that he was allowed to have anything to do with Outfox.

"The Todwoods may pay your wages, Babs," Dad had said to Mum, "but the days are gone when paying your wages meant owning your body

and soul and your family too. If the lad is careful
not to get into any trouble, the Todwoods won't
bother you about it."

Haydn heard the van draw up. Dad always
picked up Mum from the Hall in the winter. It
was too dark to be safe for her walking back to
the village through the woods. Haydn was helping
Dad wash up when he heard Mum shout from
the living room. "Come quick, Todwood Hall's
on the news!" Haydn thought it would be a re-
hash of the six o'clock piece about the Meet, but
it was worse. A white-faced and furious Lady
Todwood, standing in the doorway of her eight-
eenth century mansion, was sounding off about
Outfox.

"These protesters are supposing to be so
caring," she spat, "and they go and do something
like this! Who can believe a word they say if they
behave so badly?"

The picture cut to Olivia Hamilton in the
studio, looking worried and puzzled.

"I can assure Lady Todwood that no one from
Outfox has entered Todwood Hall with our
knowledge or encouragement. I shall immediately
question all our members to see if someone has
acted off their own bat. If we do find it's anyone
from Outfox, they will be asked to leave. But I
cannot believe that any of our members would

behave in such an irresponsible and criminal way."

The report ended with a shot of police cars and fire engines outside Todwood Hall. "What was that all about?" asked Dad. "We were only there an hour or so ago. What's happened?"

"One of those anti-hunting chums of Haydn's," said Mum grimly. "They set fire to the children's bedrooms."

"No, Mum," protested Haydn. "No one in Outfox would do that! You heard Olivia. It must have been an accident."

"The police spokesman said it was arson," said Mum. "It was a bit of a coincidence that it should happen on the same day as the Hunt, wasn't it? It said on the news that you didn't manage to stop them and a fox was killed. Well, Outfox is the obvious suspect."

"But . . . ."

"Don't But me, Haydn! I'd better phone up and see if they need me back up at the Hall tonight. There'll be a right mess to clear up. You don't mind taking me, do you, love?"

That night Haydn lay awake wondering if any of the people he knew in Outfox would do such a thing. It was only a small group. The village was full of people who, even if they didn't much care for hunting, didn't want to make trouble. Most of them thought it was a rich person's sport and it didn't have anything to do with them. The people who really cared were either young, like Haydn, or from quite well-off families like Olivia, who loathed what their parents regarded as traditional and natural.

He thought of Fergus with the sad eyes and moustache, Jeff, who was in CND and Greenpeace and wore sweaters with holes in, though his dad owned half of Lincolnshire, and Celia Hobbes, who ran a sanctuary for injured badgers and foxes and was rumoured to have a brother in the House of Lords. They were all nice people and were very friendly to him. They wouldn't set fire to children's bedrooms! Even the terrible Todwood twins' bedrooms.

Francesca and Ferdinand Todwood were *not* like the people in Outfox. They were nine-year-old tyrants who had been blooded at their first hunt as soon as they were old enough to stay upright in a saddle. The village children, whether they were anti-hunting or not, were all definitely anti- the Todwood twins.

Two days later, Lady Todwood and Olivia were on the television again. A statue had toppled over the banister and nearly killed young Ferdinand. Lady Todwood looked more frightened than angry this time and Olivia looked a lot more confident. "It would be absolute nonsense to suggest one of our members would push a heavy statue on to a little boy," said Olivia firmly.

"Even if he was the most horrible maggot," said Haydn.

"Ssh!" said Mum.

"And while we are on the subject," Olivia was saying, "I can now confirm that, as I said at the time, Outfox had nothing to do with the fire at Todwood Hall, either."

"Lady Todwood," said the reporter. "Do you believe that someone is deliberately trying to kill your children?"

"Yes, I do," said Lady Todwood and burst into tears. Haydn felt quite sorry for her, particularly when the reporter asked who could possibly want the twins dead and their mother said she could think of no one. Dad switched the set off.

"I could," he said grimly. "Half the village loathes those kids like poison, but I can't imagine anyone in Monksfield actually bumping them off."

"Well, I can't say I care for them much, myself," admitted Mum. "That Francesca is a right little madam. But they are only kids. They'll grow out of it."

"I hope so," said Dad. "Ferdinand will be the next Lord Todwood and I'm glad to think I'll be pushing up the daisies by then."

Dad wasn't very happy about Mum working up at the Hall at the best of times. Now he was getting worried in case there was some sort of maniac on the loose.

The local paper soon hit on another possible explanation. Francesca's pony's girth had been cut – or "chewed through", as the paper reported – and she had come off and broken her wrist. Ferdinand's bike brakes had been tampered with and a bookshelf in his bedroom had fallen down in the middle of the night, showering him with books. Fortunately his taste was for paperback fighting fantasies or he might have had serious head injuries. The *Monksfield Monitor* decided to sell more copies by talking of poltergeists, and had a picture of the Todwood home on the front page with HAUNTED HALL? as the banner headline.

Haydn was relieved that there were no more accusations against Outfox. He was worried about Olivia. There had been an emergency meeting after the first two incidents at the Hall and she had seemed like someone possessed.

"It serves the Todwoods right," she stormed. "They love their horrid little brats, I suppose. Let them discover what it feels like to find their offspring slaughtered. It happens to the foxes every time brutes like the Todwoods go cubbing."

"I say, steady on," said Celia mildly. "If you go round talking like that, you'll get yourself arrested in no time."

Olivia passed a hand over her forehead. "I'm sorry. I don't know what came over me. I just had such a vivid picture in my mind of a vixen whose cubs had been killed. You know I'm not the bloodthirsty type, but those Todwoods do make my blood boil."

"I'll make you a cup of camomile tea," said Jeff, whose flat they were in. After that the meeting was quite normal, but Haydn felt he had seen a new Olivia, one quite capable of arson and lethal booby-traps.

It was the first week in January and the national papers were a bit short of news. One of the tabloids picked up the "haunting" of Todwood Hall, and by the end of the week the village was full of journalists. There wasn't a bed to be had at the Fox & Hounds, and enterprising villagers started putting up Bed and Breakfast signs in their front windows.

After an incident at the Hall, when the children fell through the ice on the lake and were nearly drowned, was shown on national TV, even more people began to invade Monksfield. The new crop were "paranormal investigators" and one of them was staying at Haydn's house. His friends were impressed.

"You've got a real ghostbuster staying in your spare room?" said Eddy. "Cor! Which one's he like? Ray, Peter or Egon?"

"None of them," said Haydn. "It's a woman. And she hasn't got a proton pack or any other special equipment. Just a notebook and tape recorder."

Miss Seton was writing a book about poltergeists. She was very sensible and down-to-earth and didn't really think there was one at Todwood Hall.

"But it would be a shame to miss it out when the book's so nearly finished," she explained, "so I thought I'd better look into it."

Anyone less like a ghostbuster, in her tweed suit and little green Mini, it would have been harder to imagine, but everyone liked Miss Seton. It was more than could be said for the other ghosthunters. The reporters and photographers were popular in the Fox & Hounds because they were interested in other kinds of spirits besides the one up at Todwood Hall. None of them really believed in ghosts anyway.

The paranormal investigators ranged from mediums, who tended to be middle-aged women wearing long dangly earrings and fringed shawls, to graduate students writing dissertations, who were usually men in glasses. They were all very earnest and got in people's way terribly. You couldn't go into the village shop or the garage or the church without bumping into people with notebooks asking questions.

Haydn was surprised one day to see Miss Seton interviewing Olivia Hamilton. They were sitting on the bench of the village green and Olivia was talking excitedly, the way she had that night at the Outfox meeting. She stopped abruptly when she saw Haydn. Miss Seton was looking thoughtful. Fergus was cycling by and he stopped when he saw them all. "Have you heard the latest?" he asked. "Apparently someone put a fox's brush in Francesca's underwear drawer. Her clothes were all covered in blood."

"Oh no!" said Olivia. "They'll be bound to go back to suspecting us again. I don't think I can take many more visits from policemen and roving reporters."

"I think it's time I went to Todwood Hall," said Miss Seton. "I have all the background material I need."

"They won't let you in," said Fergus. "Lord Todwood says he's had it up to here with ghost-hunters, if you'll forgive my saying it."

Miss Seton did not look worried. "I think Percy

Todwood would be very unwise not to let me into his house. After all, I am his aunt."

Haydn went with Miss Seton to Todwood Hall and so did Olivia. She wanted to tell Lord and Lady Todwood face to face that she had known nothing of the incident with the brush till Fergus told her. They found the Hall in chaos. The twins were now too scared to sleep alone in their bedrooms and were being moved into one of the spare rooms. A policeman and policewoman were going to be stationed outside their door all night. There were more policemen everywhere, and Haydn's mum was disinfecting Francesca's bedroom and chest-of-drawers. Francesca was hysterical and the doctor had been called to prescribe her a sedative. Her father was losing patience with her.

"It's not as if you haven't seen a fox's brush before," he was saying, when Miss Seton and her companions were shown into the drawing room.

"But there was so much blood!" wailed Francesca. "And I never really thought about them being part of a real animal. I never want to go hunting again!"

"Stuff and nonsense! There's nothing wrong with . . . .Good God! Aunt Drusilla! What on earth are you doing here?"

"Good afternoon, Percy. Hello, Francesca

dear. I'm sorry you've had such a shock but I hope to get to the bottom of it very soon."

Drusilla Seton was a very calming sort of person and it was just as well, because when Lord Todwood registered Olivia's presence, he became more in need of sedation than his daughter. It took a while for anyone to notice Haydn, and by then he was chatting quietly to Francesca in a corner.

"I'm staying in the boy's house," explained Drusilla. "His mother works here, you know. I thought it might be a good idea for the twins to have some company nearer their own age."

If Haydn had been asked whether he would like to play companion to either Todwood twin before, he would have thought of some very rude replies, but he'd seen his chance of converting Francesca to his views on bloodsports. By the time Miss Seton was ready to leave, Francesca had already asked Haydn if she could go badger-watching with him and Dad.

"What about your brother?" asked Haydn. "Do you think he's still keen on hunting?"

"No," said Francesca firmly. "We don't know who's been doing all this. Dad thinks it's her," she added in a whisper, looking towards Olivia. "But we don't. Still, whoever or whatever is causing it, it's put us right off the whole thing.

Ferdy would be ready to join Outfox, but Dad would have a fit!"

Lord Todwood insisted that Miss Seton should move into the Hall. "We can't have you staying as a paying guest at our cleaning lady's," he said, then, realizing that Haydn was in the room, "and perhaps this young friend of yours would like to come and stay for a couple of nights too? He seems to be having a good influence on Francesca."

Francesca winked at Haydn and he winked back.

Haydn's mum was horrified by the whole idea. "Your dressing-gown's a disgrace! I wish we'd bought you a new one for Christmas instead of those binoculars."

"Don't fuss, Babs," said Dad. "The lad won't need a dressing-gown with all the central heating they've got up there and, if he's going ghosthunting, a pair of binoculars will be much more useful." Dad's distraction technique was too successful.

"Ghosthunting! If I thought that, there'd be no way I'd let him go to the Hall. It's dangerous up there, you know. I've had to clean up after some of the things that have happened and I can tell you someone's really out to get those children."

"Don't worry," said Miss Seton, soothingly. "I'll keep an eye on him."

So, midnight found Haydn somewhere he'd never dreamed he would ever be, in a little bedroom at Todwood Hall. It was smaller than the one the twins were sleeping in. Miss Seton had a bigger one on the other side. There was a connecting door between Haydn's room and the twins'. He thought his little bedroom must once have been a dressing room for visitors. Ferdinand had asked him to leave the door open in the night. He had been just as pleased to see Haydn as Francesca had. The Todwood twins had really changed in the last few weeks. They were sound asleep now, feeling safer than they had for a long time, with the police officers outside their door and Haydn and their great-aunt on either side. Ferdinand had great faith in Great-Aunt Drusilla.

Haydn was wide awake and he guessed Miss Seton was too. He was sure something was going to happen. The air was still, but with a faint ringing noise in it, as if the night was expecting something. He got dressed again and went to look out of the window. The lawn at the back of the house was silver with frost, illuminated by bright moonlight. Suddenly he heard a high-pitched scream. He'd know that sound anywhere – a vixen. After a moment or two, he saw her, glowing red against the silver grass. She passed up the garden steps like a . . . . well, like a ghost.

Bump in the Night

Haydn was as still as if the frost had got him too. He heard the vixen's claws scrape on the stone terrace at the back of the house. He couldn't see her any more; the broad windowsill hid his view. He slid noiselessly into the twins' room. They were breathing heavily.

Haydn went over to the window. He could hear someone or something climbing up the drainpipe. He knew he should shout for the police but his voice wouldn't work. Foxes can't climb, his numb brain was trying to tell him, not like that. Then he saw there was another connecting door on the other side of the room and it was open. Miss Seton stood there in a long white nightdress. Haydn nearly swallowed his tongue, he was so startled. She put her finger to her lips. The bedroom window started to slide slowly upwards.

The room filled with the rank smell of fox. But it was a woman who slipped stealthily over the windowsill – it looked like . . . . .

"Olivia!" cried Haydn.

The spell broke. The twins woke up screaming and the police burst in through the door. They tried to handcuff Olivia but as soon as the steel touched her wrist, she became a vixen again. The policeman backed off in horror as the little fox leapt for the open door. Her fiery red tail gave off sparks that set the bedcovers alight as she streaked past. The police were so busy trying to smother the fire that they didn't try to catch her. Haydn and Miss Seton ran to the top of the stairs. Lord and Lady Todwood appeared on the landing just as the doorbell rang. Their butler, also aroused by the noise and wearing his dressing-gown, opened the door as the vixen streaked down the final flight of stairs. She sped out into the night past the astonished figure standing on the doorstep. It was Olivia Hamilton.

The policeman came running down the stairs and grabbed her. "Right then, Miss Hamilton, I arrest you for breach of the peace, arson and attempted murder!" he said bravely, clapping his handcuffs on her wrists and then staring at her as if she were a ghost.

"All I did was ring the doorbell," said Olivia.

Miss Seton got a splendid final chapter for her book on the paranormal and a title too. *The Todwood Vixen* became a bestseller and Lord Todwood became better known as Drusilla Seton's nephew than he ever was as Squire of Monksfield. Olivia Hamilton never really understood what had happened to her during those few weeks in January.

"It was as if I kept changing minds with a fox," she told Haydn.

"Not just minds," he said. "I *saw* you, remember? You were some kind of werefox."

"That wasn't me, Haydn. The vixen's ghost was using my form to do the things she couldn't do in her animal shape."

"It was pretty horrible, what she tried to do to the twins."

"Yes, it was. But it wasn't more horrible than what the Todwoods did to *her* children. Sometimes I had her memories, Haydn, and I wish I hadn't. I don't think I shall ever forget them."

The heart has gone out of the Todwood Hunt. Now that the twins have joined Outfox, Lord and Lady Todwood are thinking of going over to draghunting. The vixen's ghost has never been seen again and Olivia Hamilton has given up henna-ing her hair.

Going for a Song

I should have known it would be trouble from the start. You know the way people say that sometimes a thing is just asking to be bought? Well, that keyboard really was. And now I know why.

It was the shop we fell for first, of course. Waterbury isn't big on shops, unless you like supermarkets, estate agents and building societies. But one day, when I was walking back from school with Steeleye and Banger, we saw it in the shopping precinct, a brand new shop window full of keyboards, gleaming drumkits and white or red guitars you'd die for. Above the window, black and silver letters against a pink background spelt out the shop's name: ROCK SOLID. It was garish, tasteless and irresistible.

Every parent in Waterbury hated it and and said it "lowered the tone". They gave it six months. Every kid from about eight to thirty-eight adored it and it soon became the biggest hang-out place in town. It was always full after school, and on Saturday mornings you could scarcely move in there. Mind you, I don't think they *sold* much. Although they had the latest heavy rock songs always playing in the shop, they didn't do records or cassettes, only instruments.

"They" was really just this old greaser called Bruno. He must have been at least forty, because he claimed he used to be a roadie for Led Zeppelin. He certainly *looked* as if he could have been. Long brown hair in a pony tail, tattoos, and a leather waistcoat without a shirt made him simultaneously The Grown Up All Other Grown Ups Loathe on Sight, Fascinating Man With a Past to the girls, and a What I Want To Be When I Grow Up for all us boys.

Bruno was full of stories, and we all envied sixteen-year-old Pete Flack, who worked at Rock Solid on Saturdays. It was the dream of every red-blooded male in Waterbury to get a Saturday job at Rock Solid. Poor old Pete Flack never knew the many sticky ends that boys not tall enough to see over the counter had planned for him in their fantasies. And in the meantime, while we all waited to be old enough, we saved our pocket money, cleaned cars and cajoled our parents so that we'd have enough money to buy something from Bruno.

But wishing didn't pay the rent and rates, and Bruno eventually had to start selling second-hand stuff too. That gave him the opportunity for more stories, of course.

"You see this guitar? Slash learned to play on this baby. I could get thousands for it as memorabilia. But an instrument like this, it's gotta be played, not stuck in a glass case in some American-style restaurant. It's going for a song now."

It was quite amazing the number of instruments Bruno got hold of that had once belonged to famous members of Heavy Metal bands. We used to stare at them open-mouthed and, if he was feeling in a very generous mood, he might let you hold the sacred relic for a few moments. We were hooked. Steeleye had his eye on a white Strato-caster, Banger was after a second-hand drumkit that had MEDALLION emblazed in gold on the bass – and then I saw the keyboard.

You might think that one keyboard looks much like another – a lot of black and white keys on a stand like an ironing board and a whole lot of knobs and buttons to make it sound like every other instrument ever invented. This one was just like that but it also had a pattern of silver snakes all over it – a bit like Bruno's tattoos, actually – and then again it had once belonged to Pit Viper.

What? You've never heard of him? Or his band, Venom? Well, to be honest, neither had we. But after weeks of hearing Bruno's stories about them, we felt deep contempt for anyone who had never heard of the Viper.

"Cut down in his prime," Bruno would say, reverently placing his long tobacco-stained fingers on the keys. "Off the back of his Harley-Davison and into a tree. You can't survive a headbanging like that."

Could he play us one of Venom's records? No, he couldn't. That was what was so tragic. Pit Viper had been on his way to cut his first single when the motorbike accident happened. It was his chance for the big time and he should have ended up in the stratosphere. "Well, maybe he did," Bruno would say sadly, "kinda."

I was hooked. For Steeleye and Banger, Venom was just another band, one whose songs they'd never hear. They were more interested in Bruno's stories about Pig Iron and Red Meat, whose records he played and whose bands, coincidentally, the Fender and the drumkit had belonged to. But I couldn't think of anything but the Viper and his keyboard. Bruno would plug it in for me and let me try it. He knew I was really interested. "Going for a song," he'd say. "Only two hundred and fifty quid."

Some song! But I was soon working out how to afford it. I still had my Christmas money and some savings in the building society. My birthday was in two weeks and if I could only get all my relations to club together, I'd have just enough.

You can imagine the conversation we had at home.

"But Alex," said Dad, "you can get a brand new electric keyboard for £199 – I've seen them in Birmingham."

I wish they wouldn't call me Alex. I mean, I know it's my name and all that, but I've asked them hundreds of times to remember that I'm called Axel now. They never do, though.

"Besides, it's not as if you'd be able to play it, without lessons," said Mum, "and where's the money going to come from for that?"

"Bruno will show me," I said. Wrong move. My parents were fully paid-up members of the Anti-Bruno Party. Mum screwed up her mouth in disapproval and Dad frowned. I plunged on regardless. "And I don't want a new one, even if it is cheaper. I want this one because it belonged to Pit Viper!"

"Who?" said Dad.

"You know, from Venom."

"Who are they?" asked Mum.

Well, I ask you! But you know they say that constant drips of water eventually wear away stone? In the next two weeks I became the world's most Constant Drip. It worked. They said they'd better give in if they were ever to get any peace. Peace! Little did they know.

"Close thing, there, Axel, old son," said Bruno, the day I went in with the money. That was another good thing about Bruno – he always called you what you wanted to be called. "Nearly sold it yesterday to a guy from London. But he tried to beat me down on the price and I knew he wasn't a real fan." Thank goodness I hadn't asked for a discount! Though I had been sort of hoping for a bit left over to spend on cassettes. I handed over all the lovely notes, Steeleye and Banger looking respectfully on. I was the first of the three of us to get his dream. Bruno gave me a receipt and promised to deliver the keyboard after he'd shut up shop.

I can't tell you what it was like to have Bruno in our house. My parents were never rude to anyone, but you could see it nearly killed my mum to offer him a cup of tea while he set the machine up for me. I think she half-expected him to take out a hip-flask and waggle it in her face, but he only said thank you, that would be very nice, two sugars please.

While he was wiring the plugs, my older sister Linda just happened to wander into my room. Bruno was as fascinating to fifteen-year-old girls as he was repulsive to parents. I couldn't get her out, and soon he was telling *her* about Pit Viper and Venom. My sister Linda! I mean, she listens to stuff like Jason Donovan! But you'd never have guessed she wasn't a seasoned metal head from the way she listened to Bruno's every word. Well, he finished setting up the keyboard and amplifier, showed me what all the buttons did, drank his tea without spilling any of it and left, throwing Dad a salute as he went.

And then I was alone in my room with it. It looked right at home against the wall where all my posters were. I wished I had a picture of Pit Viper and Venom. I started doodling on the keys. There were some great buttons for laying down heavy rock rhythms. It was all computerised, and much better quality than any of the cheap new models Dad had wanted me to buy. There was this red button right where the biggest snake's eye would have been and I couldn't remember what it was for, though I was sure Bruno had explained everything. I pressed it, and then nearly jumped out of my skin as a high wailing voice sang out over the rhythm track.

"Woh-oh-oh-oh-oh!" it went. "Yeah-eah-eah-eah-eah."

Who could it be but the Viper? Maybe it was the very track he had been on his way to cut when he was killed.

Then I had to press the "stop" button, because Mum was calling me for supper.

I bolted my sausage and chips so fast I could still feel them burning in my stomach when I raced back to my room. I was dying to tell the boys, or Bruno, but first I wanted to hear the song all the way through and write down the words. It went like this:-

Woh-oh-oh-oh-oh
Yeah-eah-eah-eah-eah.
Don't try to get away, baby
I got you in my coils.
Gonna hug you, squeeze you, bite you
Cause I'm the Snakeman.
Aaargh!

Struggle all you like
I'm gonna hold you real tight,
Gonna hug you, squeeze you, bite you,

Cause I'm the Snakeman.
Eeeegh!

People say you oughta leave me alone
I'm not a boy from a respectable home
People say I just didn't know what is right
But I don't care, now I am holding you tight.
Hissssss!

Come on, baby, settle down in my cave
Let the Snakeman teach you just how to rave
Gonna hug you, squeeze you, bite you,
Cause I'm the Snakeman.
Aaargh!

Woh-oh-oh-oh-oh!
Yeah-eah-eah-eah-eah!
I'm the Snakeman
Aaargh!
I'm the Snakeman
Hissss!
(etc. till fade)

Heavy stuff! I was shaking with excitement by
the time the track faded. Not only had I heard
the Viper's voice, I had a full copy of the single
that was never made! I was going to be rich! I
couldn't wait to tell Steeleye and Banger – I knew

they'd be green with envy. I just couldn't get to sleep that night. Funnily enough, I didn't find it at all spooky that first time, hearing a dead man's voice.

It wasn't until I told Bruno at Rock Solid after school next day that I got the first prickle of a sensation that something wasn't quite right. When I told him what I'd found, he went white as a sheet under his stubble.

"Don't you think the newspapers would be interested?" said Steeleye.

"Yeah, and the TV," added Banger. "It's a real scoop, isn't it? The only recording of the man who would have been a star."

"I shouldn't think anyone would be interested," said Bruno. "I mean, no one's heard of Venom except those of us who were at their gigs. They only played together about half a dozen times in public."

"But what happened to the rest of the band?" I asked. "Wouldn't they like to know what I've got?"

Bruno looked shifty and frightened at the same time. "Perhaps I'd better hear it first," he suggested.

So that evening back he came to our house. The boys were already there. I had to tell Mum there was something wrong with the keyboard to explain

Bruno's visit. I didn't want her to know what I'd heard yet. She wasn't happy all the same.

"Alex spent every penny he had on that machine, Mr . . . . whatever your name is. You'd better put it right straightaway or take it back to your shop and give him a full refund!"

Bruno just nodded. He looked really rattled. Mum flounced off without offering him a cup of tea this time. But Linda turned up just as coincidentally as the evening before. So there were five of us sitting on the floor and the bed of my room when I pressed the snake-eye button.

"Woh-oh-oh-oh-oh!"

The eerie high-pitched voice echoed round the room, and I felt the hair on my arms beginning to rise. When the song faded away, everyone was very quiet.

"Was that how he used to sound?" I asked Bruno.

Bruno just sat there, leaning against the side of my bed, his eyes closed, looking very pale. Then I realized why.

"Sorry, mate," I said. "He was a friend of yours. It must be a bit spooky hearing him again. Sort of voice from beyond the grave, like."

Bruno opened his eyes. "Yeah, that's just it," he said quickly. "It sort of freaked me, hearing the old Snakeman doing his favourite number

71

again. Listen, guys, if you don't mind, I'd like to go away and think about this for a while. I'll be in touch. Hang loose, man!"

Then he gave a vague, general wave and was gone. We looked at one another open-mouthed. This wasn't the Bruno we knew. That song had really got to him. It had got to Linda too. "That was great!" she said. "What did he look like, this Pit Viper? I bet he was all tattoos and muscles – really hunky!"

We all looked disgustedly at her but at least she'd liked the track. So had Steeleye and Banger. After Bruno had left, we talked excitedly about the publicity and the money.

"You should get back the quarter of a grand you paid out for the keyboard, anyway," said Banger.

"Yeah, but that doesn't matter," I heard myself saying to my surprise.

"What matters is to get the Snakeman heard."

Well, he was heard all right. After that night, I could never get the keyboard to play anything else. I suppose, looking at it rationally, the red button must have got stuck, or rather something in the machine that linked up to it. But whenever I switched it on, no matter what buttons or keys I pressed, all I got was Pit Viper and the Snakeman song. It started getting to me. I mean, it was good heavy metal stuff and those lyrics are often a bit, well, sinister, if you really listen to them, but you don't usually, do you? You just play air guitar, head-bang and go aaargh! That's what that kind of music is for, not listening carefully to the words and analysing what they mean.

But now I had a real problem. The keyboard really did need fixing, and I'd already told Mum that Bruno had put it right. And that was only part of it. When we stopped by Rock Solid the day after I played everyone the track for the first time, it was closed! There was a sign on the door, saying:

SORRY, CALLED AWAY ON URGENT BUSINESS
– CLOSED TILL FURTHER NOTICE
B BROWN (Proprietor).

Now I was really in trouble. If anyone told my parents and they found out the keyboard wasn't working properly, they'd be sure Bruno had done a moonlight. The only thing that consoled us was that all the gear was still in the shop, behind the metal grille. Bruno wouldn't abandon his stock; we were sure he would be back.

And he was, about a week later. Only, he didn't look like the same person any more. He'd had a haircut and a shave and he was wearing a clean blue T-shirt and new jeans without rips. The worse thing was, his tattoos had gone! You could see his arms looked a bit red and sore, but there wasn't a snake left on them. He'd given up smoking, too and was as jittery as anything.

He was even more jumpy when I told him the keyboard now wouldn't play anything but the Pit Viper song. His eyes looked what I can only describe as haunted. Perhaps that was what put me on the right track.

Fortunately, Mum hadn't found out about the shop being closed. She and Dad *had* noticed that I'd stopped playing on the keyboard though. There were lots of sarky comments about "told you so" and "nine days' wonder", all meaning, "He's wasted all his money on a toy he's already tired of". But what could I do? I couldn't tell them I thought the keyboard was haunted, could I? But that's what I was beginning to believe. There was that singer and that song and they had both been killed before they'd had their big chance. Bruno knew something about them that made him so scared he wanted to stop looking like a Hard Rocker. I decided I had to ask him what it was.

Linda surprised me by coming with me. She hadn't been in Rock Solid before, saying she didn't like the kind of greasy kids in leather jackets who hung out there. But she liked Bruno, even in his new cleaned-up look. While she gave her best impression of an airhead groupie, I confronted him with my ghost theory. He gave me a really ghastly smile and then stared past me at something behind me and fainted, right into Linda's arms. I turned round, fully expecting to see the ghost of Pit Viper come to get me or Bruno or at least demand that we got his song released to the public.

Instead I found my eyes almost level with the paunch of a red-headed old rocker of about Bruno's vintage. He leant over, all concern, and I saw the snakes coiling round his forearms, but he was far too solid to be a ghost.

"Come on, old son," he said, propping Bruno up and fanning him with his leather jacket. "I knew you'd be surprised to see me again, but I never expected you to keel over!"

Bruno's eyelids fluttered open. "Copperhead," he said faintly, "I would have known you anywhere."

"The very same," said the red-haired giant. "Can't say the same for you, Bruno. What's happened to you? You look like something off Blue Peter!"

He looked at Linda and me and must have reckoned we were Bruno's friends, from the way she was stroking his forehead.

"Bruno and me go back a long way," he said. "Used to be in a band together."

"Don't tell me," I said. "I bet it was called Venom."

"He's told you about us, then?" said Copperhead, who seemed quite a nice bloke when you got used to the size of him.

"A bit," I said, sarcastically. "Only he never said he was one of you." I don't know why but I had stopped feeling scared and was beginning to feel angry instead. It occurred to me that Bruno must have known there was something suspicious about that instrument when he sold it to me. He was sitting up now and the colour was coming back into his face. He struggled to his feet and looked round the shop. There were quite a few people there besides me and Linda and Copperhead, and he politely told them he was closing early. He showed them out and turned the sign round on the door. We got a few dirty looks, I can tell you. But even though I was annoyed with Bruno, I knew my street cred at Waterbury Juniors had just gone up so many notches I would never again have to worry about what trainers I wore.

"Nice little set-up you got here," said Copperhead approvingly, plugging in a Jackson Stealth and playing a few riffs, quite well. "Now all we need is someone on the drums and we could re-form Venom here and now."

"What, without Pit Viper?" I said, before I could stop myself.

Copperhead gawped. Then Bruno said quietly, "I was Pit Viper, Alex."

That was it. When he used my real name, I knew he wasn't kidding. It was as if he was saying, "let's stop pretending".

"But you told us he was dead!" protested Linda.

"Yeah!" said Bruno. "Well, he is, in a manner of speaking. There's no going back to being Pit Viper for me. I just couldn't hack it. Venom split up after half a dozen gigs and we all went our separate ways. I roadied for Led Zeppelin, Copperhead here started a computer business, Sidewinder joined another band in Amsterdam and I never heard from any of the others again. I'm afraid I spun Alex a line to make him buy the keyboard."

"But what about the song?" I said stupidly. "It was really good, a great metal classic. If you *didn't* come off your bike, why didn't you record it?"

Copperhead looked interested.

"What song? We never had our own song. We just covered other bands. That was the trouble.

We couldn't come up with any original material, so we just sort of fell apart."

"But Alex's got this song on his keyboard, the one Bruno sold him," said Linda. "It's really creepy, all about a man who's a snake, I love it."

Copperhead looked hard at us both. "Bruno sold you his keyboard, the one with all the snakes on it?"

"Yes."

He shook his head. "If Bruno parted with that keyboard, then I tell you, old son, Pit Viper really is dead."

Then Bruno said, "Maybe so. The trouble is, I never wrote that song or sang it. I didn't put it on the keyboard."

No wonder he was spooked when I played it to him! Copperhead didn't seem to understand, but then he hadn't heard the track. Linda and I just sat there like frightened rabbits.

"It was the keyboard that gave me the idea for Venom," Bruno said eventually. "All the snakes. I bought it second-hand, you see, from a shop a bit like this."

"Yeah," said Copperhead. "I remember. That was when we all went and got ourselves tattooed."

"Only I never told you the truth about why I decided to give the band up," said Bruno, looking at the red marks on his arms. "It was that song. I heard it on the keyboard and it began to haunt me. It wouldn't play anything else! It was as if someone was trying to take me over, make me perform the song. It was driving me mad. In the end I had to get away from Venom and Pit Viper. I put the keyboard into storage and it was there for nearly twenty years before Alex bought it. I thought it would have given up the ghost by now, if you see what I mean."

"So who was it?" I asked "Who was the Snakeman?"

Bruno shook his head. "I don't know. But I'd bet my Harley-Davidson he's not alive and well and living in Waterbury."

Rock Solid is permanently closed now. Bruno took back the keyboard and gave me £300 for it to cover my hassles, he told Mum. He sold it to Copperhead for £350. It seems to work all right for him. I think he's planning to start another group. But one thing's for sure, Bruno won't be in it. He's giving up Heavy Metal. The last time I saw him he was wearing a suit. I shouldn't wonder if he got a job in a building society. That's where my £300 is, waiting for a rainy day.

Funny thing, it seems to be all rainy days in Waterbury now Bruno and his shop have gone.

Bump in the Night

The window's covered in posters and the black and silver letters look sad. The "I" has fallen off, and it says ROCK SOL D. But it isn't, not any more, not since the Snakeman went away.

Reviving Ivy

"Last one out's a nerd!" yelled Greg, struggling down the front path with a rucksack, a sleeping bag and a carrier full of his precious Aerosmith records.

Each of the Latymers had something they didn't want to trust to the removal men. For Sarah it was her collection of owls and pigs, each one lovingly wrapped in tissue and placed carefully in the cardboard box she was hugging. She took one last look round her old room, stripped bare of its posters and books. It looked like any old room, where anyone might sleep.

"I'm not going to cry," thought Sarah. "Greg would never let me forget it." She squeezed her eyelids tight shut and thought about her new room in the house they were moving to. The house was much bigger than the old one, because Dad was going to use part of the ground floor as an office, but Sarah's new room was much the same size as this one. It had sloping ceilings because it was in the attic, an old iron fireplace, and a built-in clothes cupboard too shallow for her clothes to hang straight in.

There was something else about it too, but before Sarah could remember what it was, she heard her mother calling up that she wanted to lock up the house. Sarah went down the stairs carefully, cradling her box of ornaments. Goodbye, room. Goodbye, house. Goodbye, front garden with the rose Dad had planted when Sarah was born. Hello, back seat of car full of Greg and bundles.

"You'll have to have Monty in the back with you," said Mum.

"Where exactly do you suggest?" asked Greg in his most sarcastically patient voice.

"I'll have him," said Sarah. "You can put the cage on my lap."

By putting the box on the floor and shifting her legs to the side a bit, she managed to make a sloping lap for the cage containing the furious but silent Montmorency, a handsome black-and-white tom. "I know how you feel, Monty," she whispered, as he lashed his tail back and forth. He looked briefly up at her and hissed. Cars and cages meant only one thing to Monty – the vet. It was a good thing it was a short journey to the new house.

"I don't know why everyone always calls it the *new* house", Greg objected. "It's much older than our old house – Victorian at least."

"Actually it's Edwardian," said Dad. "Built along with the rest of the terrace, in 1907, six years after the old Queen died."

"Very new, very modern," snorted Greg. "That's even before Grandma was born."

"It was, in its day, the very latest design. Inside loo, piped gas-lighting, coal-fires with properly balanced flues – everything the most up-to-date from attic to cellar."

You couldn't get far with this sort of of silly argument when your father was an architect and your mother a history teacher.

"What sort of family would have lived there in 1907?" asked Sarah suddenly.

"Oh, people like us," said her mother. "A doctor and his family, perhaps, or a lawyer."

"Would he have had his surgery or whatever there, like Dad?" asked Greg.

"No. Wouldn't have had the room," said Dad,

turning into their new road.

"But there's masses of room," objected Greg.

"Don't forget they had bigger families in those days," said Mum.

"Not to mention a couple of live-in servants at least," said Dad.

"Which in our case we have not got," said Mum, climbing out, clutching her handbag, briefcase and two carrier bags full of photo albums. "So look lively, you two – there's plenty for everyone to do."

Six hours later, when the removal men had gone, they gathered, dirty and exhausted, round their old dining-table in their "new" house for their first proper meal – spaghetti and sauce. Mum and Dad drank red wine and they had candles, not to be romantic but because there had been a muddle with the electricity board and the man hadn't come to turn the electric supply on.

"Thank goodness we cook on gas," said Mum for the umpteenth time.

"Pity about the hot water, though," said Dad. "We look as if we could all do with a bath."

"I'm too tired to have a bath anyway," yawned Greg. "I'll go to bed filthy."

"That'll make a change," said Sarah, but her heart wasn't really in starting an argument. She liked the candles. She cleaned her teeth by candlelight and Mum gave her one in a saucer to carry flickering up the stairs to bed. It was eerie but rather exciting. She kept thinking what the house would have been like by gaslight; Dad had showed her the remains of the old gas mantles on various walls.

Her room was full of tea-chests and strange shadows leaping and wavering in the candlelight. Her bed was made because Mum had read somewhere that bedmaking was the first thing you should do in a new house, because you would all be too tired to do it at bedtime. There was a lump in Sarah's bed, which turned out to be a confused and bitter Monty. But going to bed was something he fully understood, and when Sarah had struggled out of her clothes and changed into her nightshirt, he consented to sit on her chest and be stroked. Sarah fell asleep to his warm purr and the guttering of the candle. Just before she lost consciousness, she thought about being a servant sleeping in this attic room and wondered what women had lived there.

She woke early the next morning to a bright light, as all the electrics snapped on. A lot of the switches and plugs had been turned on uselessly the night before, so her ceiling light and her bedside lamp had both sprung into life. The anglepoise shone straight into her face. She sat upright, wide awake, and noticed that the candle hadn't burnt down. It had been neatly snuffed and the snuffer left on on the saucer beside it. It was a little metal cone on a handle, like a wizard's teaspoon. Must be one of Mum's bits of old junk, thought Sarah, but it was funny she hadn't remembered seeing it last night or hearing Mum come in to use it; that was it – she must have brought it with her. Sarah's arms ached and her hair felt stiff and sticky. At least there could be some washing now that the electricity was on.

"What did they use to heat the water if they only had gas?" she asked Dad while she ate breakfast. He was connecting a fan extractor above the cooking hob.

"I expect they had a gas ascot in the bathroom," he said. "A sort of boiler. But all the cooking and washing-up water would have come from the range down in the old kitchen, and that would have been coal-fired."

"Sounds like hard work," said Greg, "running a house eighty-five years ago."

"It still is," said Mum. "We'll be able to have hot water in a quarter of an hour, thanks to the immersion heater, but since no robot is going to unpack all those tea-chests, I want you and Sarah to put your rooms to rights straight after breakfast."

Reviving Ivy

Sarah's room got a lot worse before it got better. Every tea-chest contained clothes, books, ornaments and shoes and almost everything was wrapped in layers of newspaper. And then there were the owls and pigs who added their own sea of tissue paper to the general mess. Fortunately her chest-of-drawers and bookcases had already been put in the room by the removal men. As she unpacked, Sarah had the strangest feeling that there was someone watching her. She was quite relieved to discover Monty on top of her built-in wardrobe.

"It looks as bad as mine," said Greg, popping his head round the door. He had the other attic bedroom, next door. They were a floor and a half away from their parents' room, and the only other room on the attic level was a tiny boxroom that Dad was going to convert into a bathroom just for the children.

Sarah and Greg decided that the only thing to do with all the newspaper was to stuff it back in the chests, which they lugged down to the half-landing, outside what was going to be Mum's study. Once that was done, Sarah's room looked quite tidy and Greg's looked like his room in their old home.

"Don't say you've started collecting junk like Mum," said Greg, pointing at a small picture

87

above Sarah's bed. It was a child's sampler, worked in cross-stitch, with all the letters of the alphabet at the bottom and a house with "HOME SWEET HOME" embroidered rather crookedly at the top.

"It's not mine," said Sarah, "I've never seen it before. It wasn't there a minute ago."

"Aha!" said Greg, crossing his eyes and waggling his fingers. "'Tis the ghost of a terrible picture came back to haunt the wall it first hung on. It'll be warming pans and suits of armour next – mark my words."

"It must be something Mum thought I'd like," said Sarah. "I wish she wouldn't keep doing that without asking." The little brass candle-snuffer was still on her bedside table.

"You've got to be firm with her," said Greg in a normal voice. "It's bad enough having aspidistras in decorated chamber-pots in the living-room. But if you once let her loose in your room, you won't be able to move for spindly-legged washstands and bamboo whatnots for knick-knacks." He mooched back to his room to stick up Aerosmith posters and put up the sign on his door which read: PLEASE KNOCK BEFORE GOING AWAY.

Sarah stared at the sampler; it looked real enough. She climbed on to the bed and reached out to touch the bamboo frame hesitantly.

"Cheek, I call it," said a voice behind her. "What's 'terrible' about that? I got 'very good' for embroidering at Mrs Wix's."

Sarah turned and saw a girl of about her own size, though obviously older. She was wearing a long brown dress, with a white apron that almost covered it and a cap over bright brown curls. She was standing on the other side of the room from the door and hadn't been there when Sarah was talking to Greg. But she looked solid enough, holding a feather duster, and with a smut on her forehead.

"Who are you?" said Sarah, wondering why she didn't exactly feel scared.

"Ivy's my name," said the girl. "And if you don't mind, I'll take the weight off me feet. That is, if that thing's supposed to be a chair."

"That thing" was Sarah's Coca-Cola beanbag and Ivy disappeared rather suddenly into it. She righted herself and adjusted her cap, looking expectantly at Sarah.

"I'm Sarah," she began.

"I know that," said Ivy contemptuously, looking round the room. "And the new master and mistress is Mr and Mrs Latymer. But when's your servants going to arrive?"

"We haven't got any," said Sarah. "Nobody

does nowadays except people living in stately homes."

Ivy sniffed. "I don't know what they may be, but I do know you can't run a home this size, stately or not, without help. Who's going to light the fires, draw the water, do the cooking, cleaning and all the laundry and ironing?"

"Well," said Sarah. "We've got central heating and the water comes out of the tap, at least it does now, and Bridget, who used to clean for us at our old house is still going to come in to do the vacuuming and ironing. And we've got a washing machine and tumble dryer downstairs in the utility room. But Mum generally does most of the cooking, though Dad always makes Sunday lunch."

Ivy looked at her, eyes as big as saucers.

"The master cooks the Sunday lunch?" she said, as if Sarah had said he flew out of the window on a broomstick. "Well, I never."

It occurred to Sarah that she was talking to Ivy in the way that she recently had to write a story at school about describing life on earth to a Martian.

"But who are you?" she said. "I don't mean your name. I mean, where did you come from?"

"Under a gooseberry bush," said Ivy promptly, snorting with laughter till her cheeks turned to pink under her brown curls. She started to choke then and to cough most alarmingly. "Only my little joke," she said, gasping for breath and smoothing down her apron. "I come from here, leastways, I came here at the beginning of the War. Lived in Hackney with me mum and dad before then. And all me little brothers and sisters."

"What war?" said Sarah. "I don't understand – you can't still live here. We've just bought the house."

"Don't I know it!" said Ivy, jumping up and starting to dust the elephants. "You're not the first by a long chalk since my day. But you're the first with any idea how to live in it. As soon as I saw the candles and the aspidistras – though you must tell the mistress them ain't flower pots she's got 'em in – I thought 'this lot'll do'."

"Do for what?" asked Sarah, bewildered.

"Company," said Ivy promptly. "I been lonely here since the War ended and everthing changed. What war? she says. The Great one of course! Wasn't I glad all me brothers was younger than me! Too little to fight, even at the end. But they got two of me uncles and me dad's best mate. Got me in the end, an' all," she muttered, sniffing into a large cloth handkerchief.

Sarah was gripping the sides of her bed with

Bump in the Night

clammy hands. She swallowed.

"Are you a ghost?"

Ivy gave her one of the dismissive looks she was getting used to.

"Course I am! Didn't they teach you anything at school? I was twelve when the War broke out and sixteen when it ended. And I'm still sixteen – so what does that tell you?"

"You're dead," said Sarah.

"Give the girl a coconut," said Ivy with satisfaction.

"Killed in the war?" asked Sarah, having a sudden vision of Ivy going off to menace the Kaiser with her feather duster.

"By the in-flew-en-zer," said Ivy dramatically, coughing a little to add to the effect.

"But people don't die of flu," said Sarah, "they, they. . . go to bed with a hot water bottle and a lemon drink."

There was an uncomfortable pause while Ivy glared. "I should think a body is entitled to know what she died of," she said eventually, rather acidly, "particularly, since I done it *in this very room* !"

Sarah shuddered. "This was your room?"

"Still is, in a manner of speaking," said Ivy. "I shared it with Mrs Potts the cook. Maud, her name was, only I had to say 'Mrs Potts', being only the general maid, though I did see her put her curlers in and take her teeth out every night."

Sarah was getting used to Ivy's way of speaking and did not let herself be diverted.

"You mean you came to work here as a maid when you were only twelve? What about school?"

"You were supposed to go to school till you were fourteen, but I was big for me age and being the oldest I knew quite a lot about housework. My parents needed the money and I got fed well here. Mrs Potts was a good cook and there was always plenty."

Sarah had a worrying thought. "What happened to her?" She didn't want two ghosts sharing her room.

"Dunno. I think she left after the war. I think the Harveys must've sold up then and the first lot of new people moved in. I didn't hang around much in the early days; you know how it is."

Sarah didn't, never having been dead, but she didn't like to say so. She wasn't scared of Ivy at all and she didn't want her to go away. She wanted to be careful not to offend her, so she just nodded sympathetically.

"Who slept in Greg's room?" she asked.

"You mean 'whose room is Greg sleeping in' really," said Ivy. "That was Jem, the general man. He did the garden and most of the heavy work, like getting the coal up from the cellar. Did all the messages too and then he had to learn to drive when the Master got his first car. That was a laugh."

"What was it like?" asked Sarah. "I mean, was it hard work? Mum says it was. Did you have any friends your own age?" She thought of leaving school at twelve, which was her own age, and leaving your parents and going to work for someone you didn't know, living in their house and sharing a room with an elderly cook.

Ivy snorted. "Didn't have time for no friends. Only got me Sunday afternoons off and went home to Hackney then. Weren't allowed followers, even though that Harry, the butcher's boy, always made eyes at me. But there was the children, little Phyllis and Cecil." Her eyes misted over. "I loved them little mites. They was just like me own brothers and sisters."

Sarah heard her mother yelling "Lunch!" from the stairwell.

"I'll have to go," she said. "Will you be here when I get back?"

"I'll come with you," said Ivy, "I'd like to see what the new Mistress is doing to the house."

"There you are," said Mum as Sarah walked slowly into the kitchen. She seemed to look straight through Ivy, who came in much more briskly and made a frank inspection of everything in the kitchen, including the canned soup heating up on the hob.

Mum took a basket of hot rolls from the microwave and set them down on the table. Everyone had two bowls of soup and a roll before starting on cheese and salad. Ivy stood by the window grinning, but apparently no one but Sarah could see her.

"Eat up, Sarah," said Dad, offering her the salad bowl for the third time. "You need to keep your strength up for all the unpacking."

The kitchen was looking quite homely. All the china had been put on the dresser and the cooking pots were all out. A string of garlic hung from a hook on the wall and there were even some houseplants on shelves beside herbs and spices. There were no chests or newspapers on the tiled floor. At least one room felt right. Monty thought so too. He was sitting on the windowsill, doing a survey of the garden birds. But every now and again he looked at Ivy. He seemed to be the only other one who knew she was there.

After lunch, Ivy whispered to Sarah, "Why has she put the kitchen in the spare bedroom?"

"I don't know," said Sarah. "Where was it when you were alive?"

"Downstairs, of course," said Ivy. "Next to the

dining room. In my day, only the servants ate in the kitchen."

"Well, Dad's got his office downstairs and there's a TV room and the utility," said Sarah. "Would you like to see?"

She took Ivy on a guided tour, although it was really the other way round. Ivy grumbled about all the new arrangements of rooms and seemed to think that the Latymers should live in exactly the same way as her own employers had eighty years ago. Sarah was quite relieved when, at tea time, Ivy seemed to have disappeared.

As she and Greg watched TV with large mugs of juice and big slabs of a cake that Bridget had brought round, Ivy and her vanished world seemed like a dream brought on by a history lesson and eating cheese late at night.

But that night Sarah went to bed early, checking round her room for ghosts and feeling glad that hers was a pine bed from IKEA and not the sort with a brass bedstead that Ivy must have died in. "I must have a flu jab this winter," she thought, yawning, and fell into a deep sleep.

She woke early to a heavy pressure on her feet which she thought at first was Monty, but turned out to be Ivy sitting at the bottom of the bed. She had taken her apron and cap off and brushed out her curls to a burnished halo.

"Here," she said. "Your ma's got a lot of books."

"Yes," said Sarah sleepily. "She's a teacher."

"She's got a whole room for 'em," said Ivy. "The old Master's study."

"Well, it's her study now. Where she prepares her lessons and does her marking. At least she will do, when term starts."

"I admire education, don't you?" said Ivy. "Girls didn't get much in my day. I reckon that's one thing your lot does better. You're still at school, I suppose?"

"Yes, of course. We have to stay till we're sixteen, but I'll probably do my A levels and not leave till I'm eighteen." Sarah suddenly realized that was a bit tactless, since Ivy had never been that old. She was looking thoughtful, and Sarah could see that Monty had jumped on to her lap.

"Did you say you cured the influenza with lemon juice nowadays?" said Ivy wistfully.

"I don't think you exactly *cure* it, " said Sarah, "I think you sort of look after it, with hot drinks and aspirin. And people don't die of it, at least I don't think so."

Over the next few weeks, Sarah got used to Ivy's company, her sense of humour, her continued interest in medical matters and her scorn of most modern labour-saving devices. The first day that Bridget came to clean, Sarah heard her saying to Mum, "It's no good, Julia, I know your thing about antiques, but I can't get the carpets clean with that." She had gone downstairs and seen the two women staring in amazement at an extraordinary metal contraption on a trolley with tubes and hoses that Bridget had taken out of the broom cupboard.

"But I've never seen it in my life," said Mrs Latymer. "It must have been left by the last people. I should think it might be quite valuable."

Sarah went back to her room, guessing correctly where the early vacuum cleaner had come from – the same source as the sampler and the candle-snuffer and various other knick-knacks that were accumulating in her room.

"Well?" said Ivy innocently, as they both heard the sound of the modern electric cleaner starting up. "It worked all right for me, didn't it? And I heard your ma say it was valuable."

The kitchen cupboards gradually filled up with glass rolling pins, egg-cutters, salt boxes, jelly moulds and coffee roasters. Mum usually polished them up and displayed them on the dresser, wearing a worried expression as if she couldn't remember buying them but was sure she must have. What puzzled Sarah was that everyone could see and touch Ivy's little presents from the past, but only she and Monty were aware of Ivy.

Ivy developed an interest in some neighbours when she overheard Bridget say she was going to work for a family called Harvey two doors along the road.

"They could be relatives of my Harveys, couldn't they?" she asked Sarah eagerly, and made her promise to find out.

Apart from her little eccentricities, Ivy was no problem. Sarah never asked where she slept but she was usually in "their" room when Sarah woke up. She was very good company; it was a bit like having an older sister, which was something Sarah thought she might like.

She asked Mum about the Harveys and found out that they and their family had lived in the road for generations. Mum liked the present couple, who were quite young, and invited them to tea. It was part of her continued quest for authenticity in decorating and furnishing the house.

"You wait," said Greg gloomily. "It'll be Edwardian right up to our floor. We'd better make sure Dad knows we don't want any of that wooden loo-seat nonsense in our bathroom or cracked toothmugs with brown flowers on – proper plastic and fibreglass for us."

Ivy got very excited when the Harveys came,

and kept nudging Sarah to ask more and more questions, till they started giving her funny looks. When Paul Harvey said he had inherited their house from his father Edward, who had got it in turn from *his* father Cecil, Ivy jumped up and danced so vigorously round the room that Sarah feared for all Mum's china knick-knacks.

"But why did Cecil live two doors away from his father's house?" asked Sarah, the minute they were alone in the attic.

"I dunno," said Ivy. "But it's a message of some kind, isn't it? Something is going to happen to me at last."

Privately, Sarah didn't see what would happen to someone who had been dead for over seventy years, but she didn't want to squash Ivy, who was looking so happy.

"He had a look of my little Cecil, too," she said dreamily. "Same blond curls and and chubby cheeks. Fancy his son and grandson living at No. 28 all the time I was gone."

"Thirty-two," said Sarah absently.

"Twenty-eight," said Ivy crossly. "*This* is thirty-two. I ought to know where I lived, didn't I?"

Sarah looked at her hard. "Ivy, *this* house is No. 28. The Harveys live at No. 32. That's why Mum's so interested in their house; it's the same way round as this one – No. 30 is the mirror image in between!"

There was a long silence.

"So your house and theirs look the same?"

"Identical."

"And they have two attic bedrooms at the top?"

"Yes, and the Harveys sleep in the front one. They've got lodgers downstairs."

"Oh," said Ivy crestfallen, picking at the hem of her dress.

"Ivy," said Sarah, reproachfully. "You're haunting the wrong house! You didn't die in my room at all!"

"So what?" said Ivy defiantly, "I expect lots of other people did."

"I don't care about them," said Sarah. "I don't know who they were, so it doesn't bother me."

"Aha," said Ivy. "So you do care about *me*?" Then she burst into tears. Sarah was horrified.

"It's just not fair," sobbed Ivy. "If only I'd known about the lemon juice and aspirins, I might have grown up and married the butcher's boy and had little ones of me own. And I could have had a washday machine and a tumbling drier and one of them Michael-wave ovens like your ma's got and I could've sat down of an evening and seen clever things on that picture box you watch and maybe got meself educated!"

She wailed until her handkerchief was drenched and Sarah offered her a box of tissues, which she glared at before blowing her nose loudly on one. Sarah couldn't think what to say to console her.

"Perhaps you'll be reincarnated?" she suggested at last, when Ivy had subsided into sniffs and hiccups.

"What's that when it's at home?" asked Ivy suspiciously. "I don't hold with setting fire to people, even if they're dead."

"It means coming round again," said Sarah. "Having another go at life. You know, the way some people can remember being Cleopatra or someone like that."

Ivy was shocked. "I'm not being her – she was no better than she should be, by what I've heard."

"No, you don't understand. You can't be someone who has already happened. You have to be born again as someone who hasn't happened yet."

"You mean a baby?" said Ivy. She sounded quite interested.

"Of course a baby," said Sarah impatiently. "But it's only an idea. I don't even know if it's really true, but some people believe that after you die, you get another chance at life. You forget about your old life except for sudden odd bits of memory."

Ivy had gone very still and quiet. "How do you set about getting yourself one of these real carnations then?"

"Honestly, Ivy, the things you expect me to know!" said Sarah, losing patience. "I've no idea. But my mum's got a book on reincarnation in her study. Why don't you go and read it?"

She wasn't exactly surprised that Ivy disappeared then. But this time it wasn't just one of her huffs; the days lengthened into weeks and there was still no sign of her. Sarah really missed her at first and then it was a bit like something remembered from a dream. About three months later, she was doing her homework when she suddenly realized that all the little Ivy-things had gone, even the sampler. She sighed. "I wish she had left me something to remember her by," she thought.

Later that evening, her mother said, "I've just heard some nice news. The Harveys are expecting a baby. And Linda Harvey said to me that by the time the baby's old enough to be left, perhaps you might like to do a bit of babysitting for them."

Sarah felt a tingling in her scalp.

"I wonder if it'll be a boy or a girl," mused Mrs Latymer.

But Sarah didn't wonder. She had a feeling she knew.

The Friday House

"Only one more block to go," thought Ziggy. Seven more houses. The old pushchair with the wobbly front wheel still held twelve free newspapers. It was always the same. Ziggy's round finished at No. 88, but when he pushed the last paper through its letter-box and heard the flap-plop that signed off his afternoon's work, there were always five papers left over.

At first he'd thought they were extras put in by the distributors in case some got spoilt or more people wanted copies. Ziggy had to grin at the thought of eager customers stopping him in the street: "*Would* you happen to have a spare copy of the *Advertiser*, young man? *So* kind!"

The Friday House

In reality, he had to avoid certain houses with angry notices on the door and run out of other front gardens really quickly after shoving the paper through the letter-box. There were fierce dogs, a big woman who swore at him and once chased him down the street and there was a mad old man at No. 74 who sang all the time about the war. Ziggy's favourite notice said: NO FREE PAPERS. NO ADVERTISEMENTS. NO RELIGIOUS PEOPLE. If he could ever afford to give up the free paper round, he was going to go to that house on his last Friday, ring the doorbell, present them with the five extras and say: "Drinka Pinta Milka Day, Hare Krishna, You Can't Beat the Real Thing, Jesus Loves You," and then run for his life.

They weren't all like that, though. Once, a young man clearing a lot of stuff out of his house had given Ziggy a big red floor cushion. It was a bit grubby and the stitching was coming undone, but it looked good in his room. So did the black wooden folding screen that a Japanese student had given him. People were always moving in and out of Park Road.

Number 86. Only one more to go. Ziggy checked his watch. 4.27pm. He always liked No. 88, not just because it was the last house. He'd never seen anyone in it, though he had sometimes spotted a ginger cat at the window. But it was sort of homely and old-fashioned. It had a fat white pair of eights stuck on the glass above the door. They looked as if they were made out of raw pastry, and they were the satisfying dumpy shape of two cottage loaves sitting side by side.

He imagined the family there living a very simple, gentle sort of life. There was no satellite dish, not even an old-style television aerial, come to that. He thought the owners were probably an old couple who sat in their living room in the evening, with the cat for company, listening to the radio, while the wife knitted and the husband made something out of matchsticks. Ziggy made them up to be like this even though he didn't know anyone like that at all. Funny that he never saw them if they were retired, though.

Flap-plop went the last paper. At 4.30pm exactly, Ziggy walked back down the path of No. 88 as he did every Friday and trundled the lopsided pushchair across to the next block to meet his mum.

He was too young to do the delivery on his own; you had to be thirteen. It was Mum's round really, but they did half each and shared the money. It was very little, for delivering 400 papers, but they needed all the extra they could get and it was quite companionable doing the papers together after school on Fridays. They always had something nice for supper that evening, knowing that the little brown envelope of coins would come through the letter-box of their flat the next day.

But this week's envelope had something else: a white slip saying that one of the residents of 88 Park Road had complained that they never got an *Advertiser*, and would Mrs Ziegler please be more careful in future.

"That's one of yours, isn't it, Adam?" said Mum, looking harassed. (She was the only person who ever called Ziggy by his given name.)

He was astonished. "Yeah, it's the last one on the round. I *always* leave their paper. Couldn't miss it."

"You'd better go round there straight after breakfast and sort it out," said Mum. "I don't want to lose this round. There're plenty of others who'd take it on."

Ziggy felt betrayed. How could they complain at good old No. 88? It was as if a well-loved shaggy mongrel had suddenly leapt up and bitten his nose.

But when he retraced his steps to Park Road, it was even worse. Number 88 wasn't there. At the end of the terrace, next to No. 86, was a small red block of flats. Not a new one either; the brick was weathered and dull. White letters spelt out

"Chester Court" on the front wall. Ziggy went up to the glass front door, his throat dry. There was a vertical row of six doorbells with name labels beside them. If this was the real No. 88, then he had always had the right number of papers.

Was this how it felt when you were going mad? He checked the street sign, went and looked at the other six houses in the block, wondering if he'd been delivering his mother's papers in the wrong road all the time. But no, there was the house where he had got the cushion and there was a faint sound of martial singing from the next block down. This was Park Road all right. Only what had happened to the house with the cottage-loaf numbers?

As he dragged back up the road, his friend the cushion man came out to put rubbish in his bin. He waved to Ziggy. On an impulse Ziggy stopped and asked how long he had lived in Park Road.

"Oh, nearly five years."

"And has that block of flats at the end always been there?"

"What, No. 88? Yeah, been there for years. Built in the Fifties, I think."

"Do you know what happened to the house that was there before?"

"No, not for sure. But it must have copped a bomb in the war. You can see all the way along these streets where the odd house got taken out. Lots of little flats squeezed in the gaps now."

Ziggy walked home more confused than ever. The war had ended in 1945, before even his mother had been born, but he had delivered a paper to No. 88 only yesterday and it had been a house like any other in the terrace. In the end he said nothing to his mother because he couldn't think of any way of saying what was such obvious nonsense. But all week he waited for the next Friday with a pounding heart.

It had got so bad by the time he was in the last block that his chest felt squeezed and his ears were roaring. It was like going to the dentist, only worse. Number 84, number 86, number. . . . and there it was, just like every Friday. An ordinary end of terrace house that no one would look twice at. Except a boy who thought he was going mad.

Ziggy walked slowly up the path and, gathering all his courage, rang the bell. It had a brassy sort of tinkle to it and he knew as soon as he heard its echo that the house was empty. He pushed at the letter box and peered through. The hall was not carpeted. It was covered in light brown shiny stuff which looked a bit cracked. A door at the far end opened into an old-fashioned-looking kitchen – no units or worktops, just a funny old grey enamel stove with little legs, and a wooden table. There was no one and nothing else to see, but there was a heavenly smell that made Ziggy's stomach rumble. It was birthday cake.

Ziggy's mum thought he was sickening for something. He ate hardly a thing all weekend and was very jumpy. He had shoved all six papers in the door at No. 88 and bolted down the path as if a demented dentist with a six-foot drill was at his heels. By the time Monday morning came round, he was actually relieved to be able to go to school and think about something else. But as soon as he met Dean in the playground, he knew he must tell his friend or burst.

Dean was thrilled. He hummed the tune from *The Twilight Zone*:

"Nana-nana-nana-nana! Is that weird or what? Let's go round there after school."

"You won't see anything weird," said Ziggy, "just a boring little block of flats."

"But my grandad lives in Park Road and he's lived there for yonks. I bet he remembers the old 88."

And he did. Ziggy realized with horror as Dean walked him up the path of No. 74 that his grandad was the mad old man who sang war songs. He was singing something about hanging out washing on the line when he came to the door, but Ziggy knew it was about war even though the words sounded harmless enough.

As soon as he saw Dean, the old man changed completely and didn't seem at all crazy.

"Hello, young feller-me-lad," he said. "Come to see your old grandad? That's right, come in and have a cup of tea, and your friend too."

He led the way into a perfectly normal (though a bit shabby) kitchen and put the kettle on. It was very easy to get him to talk about the war; Dean told him they were doing a project at school, which was actually quite true.

"Do you remember the house at the end of the next block, where the flats are now?" he asked the old man as soon as they were settled in his sitting room with big mugs of tea and a packet of chocolate biscuits.

"Was it hit by a bomb?" asked Ziggy.

"Doodlebug," said the old man immediately. "June 1944. One of the first. Horrible things, they were. Everybody hated them worse than the ones in the first blitz."

"Were you here when it happened?" asked Ziggy, gripping his mug hard.

The old man was offended. "What do you take me for? A bloody conchy? No, I wasn't here. I was in Italy doing me bit for King and Country and I've still got the shrapnel in me head to prove it!"

He was getting quite excited, and slopping his tea about. Dean gave Ziggy a look that said, *let me handle this*.

"Who lived at No. 88, Grandad? Do you remember that?"

"Course I do," said the old man contemptuously. "There's nothing wrong with my memory even if I have got a head full of metal. It was the Wellingtons – middle-aged couple with the one daughter – Betty, or Doreen or some such name."

"Were they there, when the doodlebug landed?" Ziggy couldn't help asking.

"Course they were. It was the little girl's birthday. Where else would they be? Four-thirty on a Friday afternoon, lovely June day, birthday tea all ready, cake with ten candles, just waiting for all the little friends to arrive. No warning, just the engine noise, then it stops and – boom!"

"You sound as if you actually saw it, Grandad," said Dean.

"It was your gran, rest her soul, that told me all the details," said the old man, with a sigh. "We wasn't long married and she was fond of that little girl, Maureen, was it?"

Ziggy felt cold. It wasn't that long since his own tenth birthday. He could see Dean was thinking the same.

"But Grandad, they told us at school that all the children were sent out of London to the country. There was a word for it."

"Evacuated," said the old man. "So they were, lots of 'em. And then towards the end they started to come back. But when Hitler sent the doodle-bugs, they shoved 'em all back out again. The little Wellington girl had only been back in London a few months. They didn't like to be separated from her, her being the only one."

They all three sat in silence.

"Course, they sent her away again after the bomb," the old man said at last. Ziggy and Dean sat bolt upright.

"What? But you said they were all killed!"

"I said no such thing. Do you think I'm mental or something? My Meg told me it was a miracle. It was half past four and everything was ready, so they all went out to the gate to look out for the party guests. Then they heard it, the doodlebug. So, being at the end of the road, they nipped round a bit sharpish to the Andersen shelter at the back before the engine cut out. They was all in it when the hit came."

"So they weren't killed?" asked Ziggy.

113

"Here, Dean," said the old man. "Is your friend a few coppers short of a bob? I'm telling you, aren't I? They was all in the shelter."

"What happened to them after that?" asked Dean.

"Well, the parents never really got over it, didn't make old bones. After the war they got a bit of compensation, 'cause old Mr Wellington owned the house, and the council built them flats."

"What happened to Maureen?" asked Ziggy.

"Who?" asked the old man. His eyes were clouding over a bit and he looked as if he was about to burst into song.

"Their daughter, Grandad," said Dean gently, "the little girl whose birthday it was."

"Oh, her. Sally, her name was. She still lives at No. 88, in one of the flats," and then he did start singing: "Sally, Sally, don't ever wander . . ."

"Come on, Zig," said Dean, "time to go. Thanks for the tea, Grandad."

"Why didn't he tell us straightaway that she lives in the flats?" said Ziggy outside.

"You can see what he's like," said Dean. "He remembers things that happened a long time ago really well but he isn't so hot on what's going on now. My mum wants him to come and live with us, but he's too independent."

"He seemed really, you know, quite with it until just before we left."

Dean looked embarrassed. "Yeah, I know. It comes and goes. It's true what he said, about getting wounded in Italy. My gran used to say he was never quite right after that. But he's got a lot worse since she died. He never did all that singing before."

"But what does it all mean?" asked Ziggy. "I swear to you that that house is always there when I do the deliveries on a Friday. And it's as solid as Chester Court is now. I mean, I push a newspaper through its letter-box, for goodness' sake! I couldn't do that if it wasn't there, could I?"

He was getting rather red in the face.

"OK, OK," said Dean. "No one said it wasn't there. Only, you have to ask yourself, is it really real?"

Ziggy looked at him hard to see if he was kidding.

"You mean, it might be a mirage, like seeing a pool of water in the desert that's really a reflection of something miles away? Or, or a hallucination, like something you see if you've got a bad temperature?"

"Maybe," said Dean. "Or there's one other possibility."

They stared at one another, then, slowly, Ziggy put into words what he had been trying not to think ever since Dean's grandad had told them about the doodlebug.

"You mean it might be the *ghost* of No. 88?"

Before Dean could answer, they both realized that they had reached Chester Court. Suddenly, Ziggy went up to the glass door and read the names on the labels. One said P. Wellington. He couldn't bear the suspense any longer. He rang the bell. Dean looked at him in horror, but it was too late. A pleasant-looking middle-aged woman was coming to the door.

"Yes?" she said, "What is it? Not bob-a-job again?"

"No," said Ziggy. "I want to talk to you about your tenth birthday."

"Well," said the woman, "you'd better come in."

Miss Wellington (her name turned out to be Pearl) was surprisingly unflustered. Ziggy poured out the whole story and she listened to every word. When he finished, she sat back and sighed.

"You don't know how often I've thought of that day, living here on my own. And these last few weeks I've thought about it even more than usual. Do you know it's nearly fifty years since the day that doodlebug destroyed my home and

116

took my birthday party with it? It will be my sixtieth birthday this Friday and I can't help looking back."

A stout ginger cat wound its way round the door. Ziggy jumped. "I've seen your cat in the window of the other house."

"Not this one," said Miss Wellington, picking him up. "The one we had then was old Marmalade. This is Pickles. I've always been fond of gingers."

"Did Marmalade . . .?"

"Oh, I had him down in the shelter with me. He knew the whine of a doodlebug."

There was silence in the little room, apart from the cat's purring.

"Miss Wellington!" said Ziggy suddenly. "Will you answer the door at four-thirty this Friday, even if you don't hear the bell? I've had an idea."

That Friday, Ziggy and his mum started the paper round a bit early and Dean helped. The pushchair was even more unwieldy than usual because it was piled with bags and packages as well as newspapers. Dean knocked on his grandad's door and Ziggy rang the cushion man's bell. They all got to No. 88 at the same time and Mrs Ziegler crossed to join them. They stood and gaped at the solid end of terrace house, which only Ziggy had seen before, apart from Dean's

117

Bump in the Night

grandfather, who hadn't seen it for over fifty years.

Ziggy looked at his watch and solemnly rang the bell. Almost immediately the door opened, Miss Wellington looked out and the lines of the house began to dissolve and shimmer around her. They solidified again into the smaller shape of the glass door of Chester Court. There was an overpoweringly delicious smell of cake, only this time it came from a box that Ziggy held open.

"Happy Birthday!" he said.

The Mail Must Get Through

One of the most annoying things about being a child, thought Rajiv, was the way you never got post. Oh, you got birthday cards and presents and money at Diwali, of course, but you didn't get regular satisfying thwacks of envelopes with your name on being pushed through the letter-box every day. His mother said it was simple; he didn't get letters because he didn't write any. His father said if Rajiv could see what was in the post *he* got every day, he wouldn't want it; it was mainly bills, charity appeals and unique opportunities to win forty thousand pounds.

"What's wrong with that?" asked Rajiv. "Forty grand sounds all right."

119

Another annoying thing about being a child was that even if you saved all your pocket money for the next ten years, until you'd stopped *being* a child, you'd be lucky if it added up to four figures, let alone five.

But his parents continued to throw their lucky numbers in the recycling bin, along with all the other junk mail.

One Saturday, when they both had to work at the hospital all morning and Rajiv was feeling sorry for himself, he picked up the usual handful of envelopes and notice one addressed to "The Occupier". Those ones always went unopened into the bin because his father said they would be from estate agents wanting them to sell their house or take-away pizza chains offering discounts. The Choudhurys had no intention of selling their house and they *never* bought take-away pizza.

"So?" thought Rajiv. "They won't want it. And I *am* the only 'Occupier' of the house at the moment." He put all the other letters on the hall table and took just that one to his room. He looked at the envelope again. There was something wrong about it. For a start it had a stamp and that kind were normally delivered by hand, not by the postman. Then the envelope was addressed in handwriting, not printed. And it looked old, really old, as if it had been written years ago, not all shiny and new and fresh from the printer. He shrugged and tore the envelope open. A musty smell entered the room like a sigh.

"Dear Rajiv," he read, and nearly fell off his chair.

"Thank you for opening this, I have tried to be delivered to this house so often and you are the first not to throw me away."

"I must be dreaming," thought Rajiv. "This is a letter from a *letter* !"

As he looked, the words faded from the page and the opening of a quite different letter appeared.

"Dear Fred, (it said).

Welcome back! I hope your <u>holiday</u> wasn't too uncomfortable. Thought you would like to know we looked after your GARDEN while you was away. We know how <u>particklier</u> you are about your <u>roses</u>, so we took good care of them, specially the <u>yellow</u> one! Always DIG-GING fertilizer into its roots. When you have got yourself settled back in, drop us a line and we'll come round for that *REUNION* we talked about before you went on your little trip. We'll all have a lot of news to <u>share</u>, won't we?

Yours as always,
Sid and Tim
PS No hard feelings?"

Rajiv looked at the letter in amazement. He hadn't imagined it. It had said his name before and now it was a personal letter to someone else. This wasn't the kind of letter you addressed to "The Occupier"! He snatched up the envelope and looked at the address again. It now said "Frederick Winter, Esq." in the same handwriting as the rest of the address, which was right for Rajiv's house. He had opened someone else's letter! But he hadn't meant to.

It was such a funny letter too, full of underlinings and exclamation marks and capital letters. But it was obviously saying something else besides the words on the page. Rajiv wondered who this Mr Winter was.

He decided to ask his parents, but when they came back in time for a very late lunch, they didn't know any more than he did.

"Just cross out the address, write "not known" and put it back in the postbox," said his father, without looking at the envelope. Rajiv hadn't admitted to opening and reading the letter. He didn't think they would believe the envelope had said something different when he first picked it up.

But Rajiv didn't want to let the letter go back into the postbox. He wandered out into the back garden. His family didn't spend much time there. His father cut the grass once a week in the summer and Rajiv was supposed to help his mother keep the weeds under control, but it didn't need a lot of attention. It was what the estate agents called a "mature" garden. He remembered that from when they'd moved in two years ago and he'd wondered what a "childish" garden would be like. "All sulky and disobedient," his mother had said, "and growing much too fast."

There was indeed a rose-bed at the bottom of the garden, as the letter had said, though that was nothing unusual in the suburbs. Rajiv looked thoughtfully at the large yellow rose bush just opening its first flowers in the middle of the bed. It was much bigger than the others; it *could* have had a lot more fertiliser than them.

"Hullo there, young feller," said a voice over the garden fence, making Rajiv jump. "Counting your greenfly, are you?"

Of course, thought Rajiv. Old Ron! He was the one to ask about Fred Winter.

"Hi, Ron," he said, walking over to the fence for a good chat. Ron was retired and a fanatical gardener. He had also lived in his house for about forty years.

"We had a letter for a man called Winter today," said Rajiv, not wasting any time. "Do you remember anyone of that name living here?"

A cautious look crept over Ron's large face. "*Fred* Winter? Why, he's been gone years. Who'd still be writing to him here?"

"He did live in this house, then? Only, the people before us were called Mulligan."

"Fred was before them," said Ron. "He moved in about five years after me and Doris."

"What happened to him?"

"What you mean, happened? He just left. Went to live with his daughter in Eastbourne, about fifteen years ago."

"Is he still alive?"

"I dunno. Could be. He'd only be a year or two older than me and I got a good few years left in me yet." Ron thumped himself heartily on the chest and coughed so much he nearly choked.

"Do you know his address in Eastbourne?" asked Rajiv, when Ron had recovered.

"I used to have it somewhere," the old man said doubtfully. "Here, tell you what. I need a cup of tea to settle my chest after all that coughing. Why don't you come round and have one with me and I'll see if I can find it."

Rajiv had often been next door. Doris made wonderful cakes, which had over the years had an effect on her husband's figure. Now he and Rajiv tucked into a plate of warm scones, dripping with butter.

"Just let me get my breath back," said Ron, "and I'll have a hunt for that address."

"What address?" asked Doris, pouring tea so strong it looked like Coca-Cola.

"You remember old Fred Winter next door?" said Ron.

Doris's mouth snapped shut like a mouse-trap.

"I think I'll go and get on with my sewing," she said, taking her tea with her. Ron sighed.

"Doris never really liked Fred," he explained. "Especially when he had that bit of trouble."

Rajiv felt the hairs on the back of his neck prickling.

"What trouble?"

Ron shifted uneasily in his chair. "Well, it can't hurt to tell you now, I suppose. I'm afraid Fred was a bit of a bad 'un. Easily led perhaps, but he fell in with a bad lot and ended up in prison."

"Why? What did he do?"

"He and two other blokes robbed a mail van. They were only petty criminals really, after postal orders and kids' birthday money. A nasty, mean little crime and they deserved to go to prison. Trouble was, they got more than they bargained for. Have another scone."

Rajiv nearly choked he ate his scone so fast. This was more like it! To think of a robber living in their house! "What do you mean, they got more than they bargained for?" he said eagerly.

"What? Oh, more money for a start. That particular van was carrying a load of cash, as well as the usual sacks of letters. It shouldn't have been. It was all very irregular but it was twenty odd years ago, before they went in for all these security guards and vans. The usual van for delivering money to all the branch post offices had broken down and the mail van driver had agreed to carry it in his."

"How much?" asked Rajiv.

"About fifty thousand pounds altogether," said Ron.

"Wow!"

"And of course that was worth a lot more then than it is now. We're talking about the time when a thousand pounds a year was a good salary. Fred certainly never earned as much as twenty quid a week by honest means."

"But he got caught, didn't he?" asked Rajiv. "You said he went to prison."

"There was a scuffle," said Ron. "The van driver hung on to Fred like grim death, but the other two escaped with the sacks. Shoved them all into their Capri, money, letters and all and did a bunk. But a woman in a house nearby saw everything and called the police. They got there really quickly and found Fred and the driver still slogging it out."

Rajiv suddenly had an idea.

"Ron," he asked, "how come you know so much about it?"

"I was the driver," said Ron quietly.

There was silence in the little room apart from the ticking of the clock.

"It wasn't the money," Ron continued. "Not so much. It was the thought of all those letters not reaching people. Letters change people's lives, you know. A letter saying 'goodbye', or 'I love you' or 'sorry' or offering some hardworking kid a place at university or telling someone they've won the pools. The mail must get through, that's what they always told us at the post office. So I made sure I caught one of the robbers. I didn't know it was Fred then, though. They were all wearing balaclavas. But that was the first thing the police did, pulled his balaclava off, and I identified him."

"What happened then?" asked Rajiv.

Bump in the Night

"Well, they took old Fred off to the station and charged him with robbery and assault. He didn't get bail. He was tried and found guilty and sent to prison for five years."

"What about the others? What happened to the two who ran away?"

Ron sighed. "Nothing happened to them. Fred refused to say who they were. They were never caught."

"But what about the money?"

"No one ever found out. The numbers of the notes were recorded and the police never found that anyone had tried to use any of it. The most likely thing is that the other two hid it until they thought it was safe to spend it. Most probably Fred got his share of it when he came out of jail and went to Eastbourne."

Rajiv's mind raced.

"No, Ron, I don't think he did," he said.

"What do you mean? You didn't even know who he was until today!"

Rajiv took the letter out of his pocket.

"I opened this letter, by mistake," he said and handed it to Ron.

"What do you reckon?" he asked. "Don't you think all that about Fred's 'holiday' and 'digging' and 'sharing' sounds as if they buried the money in his back garden?"

128

"Only it's not Fred's back garden, any more, is it?" said Ron. "It's your back garden." They stared at one another.

"It's nice that Rajiv gets on so well with old Ron next door, isn't it?" said Mrs Choudhury to her husband. "He spent ages round there at tea time yesterday and now Ron's helping to weed our back garden."

"Mmm," said Mr Choudhury, looking out of the window. "It looks more as if they're digging up the rose-bed to me."

"Oh I expect there's a sucker they're trying to get rid of," said his wife. "Ron knows what he's doing. His own garden always looks perfect."

"This one's got roots all the way down to Australia," grumbled Ron. "Let's take a breather."

They rested on their garden forks for a while, both trying hard to believe that there was £50,000 under the big yellow rose tree.

"Ron?" asked Rajiv. "Whose money is it? I mean if we find it, can we keep it?"

"No, I shouldn't think so," said Ron.

"You mean we'd have to give it to Fred?"

Ron snorted. "No, I do not. He's not entitled to it. I should think it's Treasure Trove or Crown Property or something."

"What if we didn't tell anyone? We could have half each!"

Twenty-five thousand pounds! It was a fortune. Rajiv thought about how he could take his whole family to India and stay in luxury hotels and still be able to afford a mountain bike *and* a TV *and* a computer when they got back. He couldn't tell what Ron was thinking; he had gone very quiet.

Eventually he straightened up. "Come on, we'd better get these cleaned up and back into the shed," he said.

"What do you mean?" asked Rajiv, horrified. "We haven't got down to the money yet."

"No," said Ron, "and I reckon we should stop before we do. Two wrongs don't make a right. That money's already been stolen once and now you're asking me to do it again. Mark my words, no good ever came of stolen money. It's got a sort of curse on it."

They stood in the warm sunshine staring at one another. "OK, Ron," said Rajiv. "You win. If we find it, we'll tell the police straightaway."

"That's my boy!" said Ron.

"Wait a minute, though," said Rajiv. "Why didn't the other two come back and dig it up and why didn't Fred get their letter when he came out of prison?"

"I just don't know," said Ron. "I've gone over

and over it in my mind. I think something must have happened to them."

"Why don't we ring Fred's daughter in Eastbourne?" asked Rajiv. "We could ask her if she knows a Sid and Tim."

"You'll have to do it," said Ron. "If Fred heard I was asking about his accomplices, I reckon he'd come back here and finish me off."

Rajiv racked his brains and decided in the end the only thing he could do would be to say that a letter had come to his house for Fred Winter and take it from there. His hands were slippery with nervousness when he picked up the phone and dialled the Eastbourne number. Ron stayed outside the sitting room door, keeping an eye out for Rajiv's parents while he made the call. It went on for a long time.

"I see. Thank you," said Rajiv, putting down the phone.

"Well?" asked Ron.

"Fred's dead," said Rajiv. "Died two years ago."

"Well, at least he can't come and do me over," said Ron.

"No, but there's more," said Rajiv. "I said a letter had come from a Sid and Tim and she went all funny and said that wasn't possible. She said they were killed in a fire in 1977."

131

"What? That was the year old Fred got out of jail!"

"Yes – she said he heard about it when he returned here after some time away. I said what a pity, he must have been very upset and *she* said, 'hopping mad was more like it'."

"I bet he was," said Ron grimly. "They were the only ones who knew where the money was. And to think it was in his own garden all the time!"

"But Ron, the funny thing was, she said they were caught in a fire in a sub-Post Office."

"What? Not the Willoughby Road fire? That was in all the papers. But the blokes who died in that were some kind of heroes!"

"She said it made the national news, being the Queen's Silver Jubilee day and all. Someone who'd had a bit too much to drink at one of the street parties dropped his cigarette and there was so much paper around, it being a newsagents as well, that it went up like a torch."

"And everyone ran out of the shop, but then someone said there were kiddies upstairs in the flat looking out the window at the procession," said Ron slowly, "and two men forced their way upstairs through the smoke to try and save them."

"And the children jumped out of the first floor window and were saved by the shop's awning," said Rajiv. "But the two men died. The whole building was ablaze by the time the firemen got there."

"And that was Sid and Tim," said Ron. "Has that letter of yours got a postmark on it?"

Slowly Rajiv drew the letter out of his pocket. He'd been pretty sure there hadn't been a postmark before, but he hadn't forgotten how strangely that letter had behaved when he first opened it, even though he had never mentioned it to Ron. It now said clearly 7.06.77. 1.15 pm.

"That's impossible," said Ron. "That's Silver Jubilee day and the fire was at midday."

"It must have been what they went out to post," said Rajiv.

"The mail must get through," said Ron softly.

After that, they decided to tell Rajiv's parents everything. It was afternoon before they all went back out to the garden. With several pairs of hands to help, it wasn't long before the big yellow rose tree lay on the lawn, waving its long roots in the air. They dug several more feet before hearing the satisfying clunk of spade on metal that all treasure seekers long for. And *that* was when they rung the police.

So there was a uniformed constable and a detective sergeant standing by to witness the strong-box being lifted out of the earth. It was all there, wads and wads of notes – twenties, tens, fives, even some ones.

"I've never seen a one pound note," whispered Rajiv. "It's funny to think that money's been there since before I was born."

Mr Choudhury had to sign something to say that the money had been recovered from his garden and the policeman gave him a receipt. Then he turned to Rajiv.

"Now, young man, could we have that letter that put you on to this in the first place?"

Rajiv put his hand in his pocket but there was nothing there. They all searched the house and garden but there was no sign of the letter; it had simply vanished into thin air. The police obviously thought it was a bit suspicious, but they weren't too worried. The main thing was that the money had been found and they didn't really think that Rajiv could have anything to do with the robbers.

"Well, that's that," said Mrs Choudhury. "I don't suppose we'll ever see so much money in one place again."

"No," said her husband, "I don't suppose we will. But maybe Rajiv will get something as a reward. What do you think, Ron?"

"I think," said the old man slowly, "that there's just the ghost of a chance he might." And he winked at Rajiv.

Things Haunt What They Used To Be

It was so hot that August that the road surface bubbled as it had on the day it was laid. The whole city smelt of petrol fumes and everyone's skin felt sticky and and gritty an hour after they'd got out of the bath. The roads to the coast were jammed every day and particularly on Saturdays, as families streamed out of the city in search of some fresh air.

But some people didn't mind not going on holiday, and Cassie was one of them. She was so used to car fumes she didn't notice them any more. Cassie lived with her dad who, with her grandad and her uncles Oliver, Oscar and Morris ran the VROOM! garage. Dad's name was Vincent and Grandad was Reginald, so it had only been a matter of time before the garage was renamed. When it had belonged to Grandad on his own it had been simply Murphy's Motors. It was Dad who had thought of VROOM! "Typical," said Uncle Oscar, "putting himself before Dad," but they all had to agree that it was the only order in which their initials made sense, and such good car sense too.

"Who does the exclamation mark stand for then?" Cassie used to ask.

"Ah, that's for you, petal," her grandad would say, picking her up and tickling her, long after she was too old for that sort of thing.

But in time everyone came to accept that Cassie would be part of the garage when she grew up. It was a funny thing. All her uncles had married and had sons long before Vince had had his disastrous short entanglement with Cassie's mum. Cassie had boy cousins old enough to be her own father, but not one of them was interested in cars. One ran a computer showroom, one was a fishmonger, one worked in a supermarket and one, the one they didn't talk about, so that Cassie didn't even know which uncle he was the son of, had run off with Cassie's mum when Cass was still in nappies. They emigrated to Australia and

none of the Murphys had ever had any contact
with them again.

Cassie didn't mind. She loved her dad, and she
was the apple of his eye. She loved her grandad
and uncles too and, though her grandma was
dead, she had three aunts-by-marriage who spoilt
her rotten. She had been a bridesmaid at her
older cousins' weddings five times already, always
had loads of presents at Christmas and felt as
much at home in her uncles' three houses as she
did in the flat over the garage where she lived
with Dad and Grandad Murphy.

And most of all she loved cars. She was the
only one of her generation who did. Dad said it
was because she had breathed in petrol fumes in
her cradle. Even before her mum ran off with
Cousin Tony, Cassie spent many hours of her
babyhood in a carrycot in the garage workshop,
while Dad worked away under some Toyota or
disappeared under the bonnet of a Renault 5.

That was the only fly in the ointment as far as
Cassie was concerned. She loved pulling on her
overalls after school and at weekends, and she
never felt happier than when the men gave her a
job to do and she went upstairs for dinner with
smears of oil on her face. But they never really
got any *classy* cars to see to in VROOM! "One

engine's much like another," Dad would say.
"Once you've seen one cylinder, you've seen them
all." But Cassie longed to see the sleek lines of a
Porsche or a Mercedes or even perhaps one day a
Lamborghini, preferably a red one.

They did occasionally get an old MG or a
Jaguar, flashy cars that did nothing for Cassie.
The garage was in the East End, but not very
handy for the docklands, and anyway everyone
said the yuppies were having to sell off their
BMWs and move out. So VROOM!, in spite of
its snazzy name, made its money out of MOTs
and repairs on family saloons, and trade-ins on
Honda hatchbacks and Ford estates.

Still, even that was more fun to Cassie than
building sandcastles on a beach with thousands of
other families, especially in August, which was
the busiest month for the garage. There were all
the people who wanted to buy cars with the new
registration letter and even more people who
wanted to buy the year-old cars that the first lot
had traded in. And it was amazing how much
work some year-old cars needed to make then
saleable at a decent price. Yes, August was the
month of sandwiches munched in oily hands and
Chinese take-away dinners eaten out of the car-
tons before flopping into bed tired and satisfied.

Cassie had just come back with a full carrier

bag from the sandwich bar at the corner when she saw it. It had been left on the forecourt with the keys in the ignition and a note under the windscreen wiper. Cassie wasn't very old but she knew a stealable car when she saw one. She took the keys and walked into the garage, feeling as if each step was buoyed up by a size nine cloud.

"Ah! Here's the girl we're all waiting for!" said Grandad, coming out of the office where he'd been doing the accounts. The four Murphy brothers emerged, hungry and grinning, from under or inside various bits of cars, wiping their hands on bits of rag so dirty it was doubtful whether anything more hygienic than an exchange of smears took place.

"What's up, pet?" said Vince. "You look as if you've seen a ghost!"

Cassie found her voice. "No, Dad, an *angel* – the most heavenly car I've ever seen and it's on our forecourt! Look, here are the keys."

Something in Cassie's face brought the whole family outside, and their open-mouthed expressions and round eyes in faces so alike made a comic sight – if there had been anyone else there to see.

"How on earth did that get there?" said Morris eventually.

"It wasn't there when I went out," said Cassie.

139

"I couldn't have missed it."

"But we never heard a car draw up," said Ollie.

"No, and no one came into the shop," agreed Oz.

Vincent just stood there whistling under his breath. It was Grandad who read the note out.

"Murphy – Have her ready for me by midday tomorrow. I'll make it worth your while."

The signature was unreadable. But nobody really cared whose car it was then. It was the kind of car you didn't really *own* anyway – it was just a privilege to know you existed on the same planet.

It was an early Rolls Royce open tourer in immaculate condition. Everything was there – spare wheel above the running board, cobra-head horn, the radiator grille like a temple, with the elegant double R in the middle of the pediment, and there, on the top of the bonnet, was the famous mascot.

"The Spirit of Ecstasy," said Vince, touching the graceful figure with the tip of one reverent finger. Grandad was the one who took the keys from Cassie and gently drove the purring Rolls into the workshop.

"We'd better be extra careful tonight," said Oz. "If anyone's seen this little beauty, we want to make sure our security is good and tight."

The Rolls sat in the middle of the workshop like the QE2 in a fishing harbour. It immediately made every other car in the garage look shoddy, even the brand new August models going out to buyers in the next few days.

"Just looking at the workmanship is a treat," sighed Ollie, running his hand over the soft black leather upholstery.

"Here, watch it!" said Morris sharply. "It's a good job that leather's black. Look at the state of your hands!"

They all looked at their own hands then and went off to get washed while Grandad locked the outer doors and Cassie brewed up a pot of tea in the office. All other work was forgotten as they sat round eating their sandwiches and staring at the Rolls. Cassie drank scalding sweet tea from her own special mug and wondered if she'd be allowed to help. It was obvious that the afternoon would be devoted to this wonderful machine.

When they'd all finished eating, Grandad flexed his long fingers like a concert pianist about to give a virtuoso recital or a brain surgeon before performing a delicate operation and said, "Gather round, lads. You are about to get the education of a lifetime."

"And me, Grandad," begged Cassie.

"Of course you, my little exclamation mark,"

said Grandad, putting his arm round her shoulders. "You found her and, what's more, you brought her keys straight in, like a sensible girl. Of course you can watch."

"Watch?" said Ollie. "Is that all we're going to do? I suppose you're going to have all the fun."

"*I'm* going to be the one taking the responsibility," said Grandad.

"Murphy, it said on the note."

"We're all called Murphy," said Vince quietly, "even my little Cass here. I reckon we should all have something we can do with a machine like this."

The stifling afternoon was turning into muggy evening when they had all finished. It had been the happiest day of Cassie's life, cleaning and oiling various bits of that precision-tooled six-cyclinder engine. The other Murphys felt the same. They had handled the Roller the same way they would have treated a visit from the Queen herself. No quarrelling, no smoking, no swearing and every operation conducted with politeness and awe. The only trouble was, they could find nothing wrong with the car at all; it was in perfect working order.

In the end, Grandad said they should just change the oil and make sure that everything was clean and the spark plugs wiped dry. Cassie had

even been sent upstairs for some old sheets to tear
into fresh rags. It was the first time she had ever
seen a clean rag in the garage, though they must
all have started out that way at some time.

The uncles dispersed to their wives and homes
and hot dinners and cold beers, leaving Grandad,
Dad and Cassie to lock up. But after a good fish
and chip supper with plenty of salt and vinegar,
Grandad said he was going back down.

"It's no good, Vince. I shan't sleep a wink up
here knowing that beauty is down in the
workshop."

"Let me go then," said Cassie's dad. "I don't
mind kipping in the office, and if villains do try
to get in, I'll be quicker to sound the alarm than
you would."

In the end, they all three spent the night in the
garage. Cassie stretched out on a workbench in
her sleeping bag with a pillow under her head
and, once she had moved a few lumpy spanners
out from under her, she had no trouble getting to
sleep. Dad and Grandad wrapped themselves in
blankets in chairs in the office. Cassie drifted off
to the sound of their low voices talking about who
the marvellous car could belong to.

The Rolls gleamed silver in the moonlight that
filtered through the skylight. The Cortinas and
Metros and Mazdas huddled into the shadows

like extras on a film-set when the big star walks in.

It was the first thing Cassie saw when she woke up. Grandad was already brewing up in the office. Everything looked strange and ordinary at the same time. She had known the garage all her life but hadn't woken up in it since she had been that baby in a carrycot. And it had never housed anything like the Rolls.

All morning, the Murphy brothers were on edge. Customers coming in to pick up or leave cars were all mesmerised by the vintage tourer. One or two of the older ones looked thoughtful, as if they could remember something about it. As midday grew closer there were fewer people around and then, suddenly, there he was in the doorway. A man in a double-breasted suit with big lapels and a broad stripe. He wore a light-coloured hat with a dark band, and had a light-coloured raincoat hanging loosely from his shoulders. He looked like every gangster in every black-and-white film Cassie had ever seen on the television of a Sunday afternoon. She expected him to have a cigarette holder and a pearl tie-pin.

He walked unhurriedly over to Grandad.

"Afternoon, Murphy," he nodded.

"Afternoon, sir. What can we do for you?"

144

stalled Grandad. Cassie knew he didn't want to part with the Rolls.

"I've come to collect my car," said the man, "this car," pointing to their pride and joy, as if he could have meant any other. He took out a bulging wallet. "How much do I owe you?"

"Well, you see, sir," said Vince. "We couldn't find anything wrong with her. We spent all yesterday afternoon going over her and I think you'll find she runs sweet as a dream."

"You're quite sure? No damage of any kind? My car has to be perfect."

"She's that all right," said Vince.

The man laughed. "Good, good. I've always trusted Murphy's Motors. You must be young Reg?"

"No, sir," said Grandad. "I'm Reg. These here are all my sons. That's Vince and that's his little 'un, Cassie."

"Cassie," said the man, looking at her. "She's a proper little grease monkey, isn't she?"

Cassie flushed. She didn't know if it was a compliment or an insult. But he had already stopped looking at her and was handing Grandad a wad of used notes, and his business card.

Then he slipped into the tourer, tossing his raincoat and soft leather gloves into the back, and man and car glided out of the garage for ever.

Grandad stood for a long time turning the oblong of pasteboard over and over in his hands. Morris broke the spell. "Go on then, tell us who he was."

"Colin Collins, it says here," said Grandad. "Security Services." He looked thoughtful.

"Don't you think it's true then?" asked Vince.

"I seem to remember a Collins from round here during the war," said Grandad.

"He didn't look that old," objected Ollie.

"That's it!" Grandad suddenly shouted. "Colgate Collins, they called him. And he did have a Roller.

"Couldn't have been," he said and suddenly sat down heavily on an oilcan, white as a sheet. "Colgate Collins was gunned down outside The Pig and Petticoat in 1947."

For the first time in its history, whether as Murphy's Motors or VROOM!, the garage sported a "CLOSED" sign on an August afternoon. Vince took them all out for lunch to the local pizza place and then said they were going to the library. Grandad was looking better now, and on the way Cassie asked why Mr Collins had been called "Colgate".

"Well, pet, he was a bit of a villain. He ran a protection racket. Do you know what that is? It

146

was part of a way of life in the East End years ago. Still goes on in some parts. Local businesses paid Collins large sums of money to make sure nothing happened to them."

"What would happen if they didn't?" asked Cassie.

"Oh, nothing much at first. A few broken windows, money out the till. But if they didn't get the message, Collins made the hints heavier. He had quite a heavy mob to help him. And eventually guns came into it."

"Did you pay him money?"

"I didn't own the garage then – I was just a young whippersnapper. My dad, your great-grandad, ran the business in the war. I don't know what arrangement he had with Collins, but nothing ever happened to the garage. I only saw Colgate once, shortly after I got back from my National Service. The war had been over for a few months."

"You haven't told me why he was called Colgate," said Cassie.

"Because he offered protection, like the toothpaste."

They arrived at the branch library and the librarian looked surprised to see so many Murphys at once. Vince asked if they could look at copies of the local newspaper from the year 1947, and the librarian brought them a large stack of yellowed *Couriers*.

They sat down at a table and each took a pile. It was Cassie who found the story; it had been front page news.

"GUNMEN KILL GANGLAND BOSS"

screamed the big black letters. There was a picture of the man in the double-breasted suit.

The Murphy family gathered round eagerly to read the story over Cassie's shoulder.

Local racketeer "Colgate" Collins (45) was shot dead by two masked gunmen as he was leaving The Pig and Petticoat pub in the High Street on Monday. The two men escaped as Collins bled to death on the pavement. They used his own Rolls Royce car for the getaway. Police gave chase and the two men drove the Rolls out of control onto the junction with Market Street and smashed into the travel agents on the corner. Both men were pronounced dead on arrival at hospital and have yet to be identified.

Mr Collins was heard by bystanders to murmur, "Not the Roller! Don't let them take the Roller!"

"It was his pride and joy that car," said Lily Devlin (23) the attractive brunette barmaid at The

Things Haunt What They Used To Be

Pig and Petticoat. Mrs Angela Collins (29) is being comforted by relatives at the racketeer's luxury twelve-bedroomed house in Esher.

There was another picture, of the pub and the pretty barmaid.

"I remember Lily Devlin," sighed Grandad. "She was a cracker. Hard to believe it was nearly fifty years ago."

"What's the date of the paper, Cass?" asked Vince.

"Thursday 7th August," read Cassie.

Grandad shook his head. "Those were hard times, just after the war. People found it hard to pay Colgate his protection money and I reckon the sight of him swanning round in that car must have been like a red rag to a bull to some people."

"But why did he bring it to us?" asked Cassie. "And why wasn't it all smashed up?"

"And why wasn't he full of holes, come to that?" asked Vince. "I can't believe that bloke today was a, a 'you-know-what'."

"I don't understand any of it," said Grandad. "Unless he can't rest in peace because he's so worried about what happened to the car. You know, sort of unfinished business."

"Like a sort of Flying Dutchman on wheels," said Ollie helpfully.

They all left the library in a quiet mood.

"No point in opening up now, is there?" said Oz.

"Why don't we all take Cassie to the pictures?"

By the time they got back to VROOM!, a fine rain was laying the dust on the pavements.

"Weather's broken at last, I think," said Vince. "It'll be cooler tonight."

But Cassie found it hard to sleep. She lay awake thinking of how "Colgate" Collins had bought that beautiful car with money that frightened people had scraped together to stop their knee-caps being shot off. And how it had ended a tangled mess of metal and bodies. Cassie thought that if it had been her car, she might have hung around garages anxiously checking it was all right too. She wondered if "Colgate" would ever rest in peace.

"Still awake, princess?" asked Grandad softly, stopping by her door.

"Yes, I can't stop thinking about that car."

"Nor can I, love. I reckon we'll never see anything like her in our garage again."

"Still, it was lovely while she was there, wasn't it?" said Cassie.

"It was. It was the most beautiful car I've ever seen," said Grandad. "I'll never forget it."

"Nor shall I," said Cassie. "Even when I get

my own Lamborghini!"

Grandad laughed. "That's my girl!" he said. "Snuggle down now, my little exclamation mark, and get your beauty sleep. There's plenty of other cars for you to work on in the morning."

And Cassie feel asleep, thinking of the Roller.

It was, of course, a Silver Ghost.

The Fairy Rebel by Lynne Reid Banks

Jan is moping in the garden when Tiki is accidentally "earthed" on her big toe. Being "earthed" for a fairy means that she can be seen, and Tiki has just broken one of the most important fairy rules. Another important rule is never to give humans magic favours, but when Tiki hears Jan's very special wish, she is determined to help, risking the Fairy Queen's fury with frightening results.

The Farthest-Away Mountain
by Lynne Reid Banks

From Dakin's bedroom window, the farthest-away mountain looks quite close. She can see the peak with its multi-coloured snow clearly, just beyond the pine wood. No one can tell her why the snow isn't white, because no one has ever been there; for though the mountain looks close, however far you travel it never gets any closer. Then one morning, Dakin is woken by a voice calling, summoning her to fight the evil on the mountain and set it free...

I, Houdini by Lynne Reid Banks

Houdini is no ordinary hamster. Like his namesake, he was born with quite exceptional talents for getting out of cages. He chews, wriggles or squeezes his way out of every cage his adoring people try to confine him to, strewing chaos, havoc and flood behind him and surviving fearful dangers.

All at £2.99

The Prism Tree by Kate Andrew
£2.75

Toby and Hardly Visible are determined to foil
Slubblejum's terrible plot to cut down the Prism Tree,
for without the Tree there would be no colour in the
world. But Toby and his friend are prisoners on the
nethercat's ship. Can they escape in time?

Black Harvest by Ann Pilling
£2.75

The ruggest west coast of Ireland seems like the perfect
place for a holiday. Then everything starts to go
wrong. Prill's dreams are haunted by a starving
woman; Baby Alison falls sick with a strange illness;
Colin is aware of an awful smell. Only Oliver, their
cousin remains unnervingly calm...

The Witch of Lagg by Ann Pilling
£2.25

The ancient castle of Lagg hides a secret, though it's
nothing as straightforward as a vampire. It's
something with a very strange power. As Colin, Prill
and Oliver explore the rambling old house and the
dark woods surrounding it, they find themselves
becoming the victims of some evil force, something full
of threat...

Vlad the Drac by Ann Jungman
£2.99

Paul and Judy are fed up with their holiday in Romania, until they find a baby vampire under a stone. They smuggle him into England, disguised as a souvenir, but all too soon the trouble starts.

Vlad the Drac Returns by Ann Jungman
£2.99

Vlad is on holiday in England, and he's bored. And whatever he starts out to do, poor old Vlad always ends up in a scrape – like the day he fell into a food mixer! Luckily Paul and Judy pick up the pieces.

Vlad the Drac Superstar by Ann Jungman
£2.99

Vlad comes to live with the Stones while he's starring in his first movie. Not only does he disrupt the whole film studio, but he becomes monstrously big for his boots at home.

Vlad the Drac Vampire by Ann Jungman
£2.99

As soon as Vlad hears about Paul and Judy's new baby sister, he comes to "help". To keep him out of mischief, Mum suggests that the children take him sightseeing – with disastrous, hilarious consequences.

ORDER FORM

To order direct from the publishers just tick the titles you want and fill in the form below:

Name _____

Address _____

_____

_____

Send to:
Department 6, HarperCollins Publishers Ltd,
Westerhill Road, Bishopbriggs, Glasgow G64 2QT

Please enclose a cheque or postal order to the value of the cover price plus:

UK & BFPO: Add £1.00 for the first book, and 25p per copy for each additional book ordered.

Overseas and Eire: Add £2.95 service charge. Books will be sent by surface mail but quotes for airmail despatch will be given on request.

A 24 hour telephone ordering service is available to Visa and Access card holders: 041-772 2281